I0682501

Who Owns the World?

The Parable of Tehya

This is her story. This is our opportunity.

By Darby Checketts

iUniverse, Inc.
New York   Bloomington

Who Owns The World?
The Parable of Tehya

Copyright © 2008 by Darby Checketts

All rights reserved. No part of this book may be used or reproduced by
any means, graphic, electronic, or mechanical, including photocopying,
recording, taping or by any information storage retrieval system without
the written permission of the publisher except in the case of brief
quotations embodied in critical articles and reviews.

iUniverse books may be ordered through booksellers or by contacting:

iUniverse
1663 Liberty Drive
Bloomington, IN 47403
www.iuniverse.com
1-800-Authors (1-800-288-4677)

Because of the dynamic nature of the Internet, any Web addresses or links
contained in this book may have changed since publication and may no
longer be valid. The views expressed in this work are solely those of the
author and do not necessarily reflect the views of the publisher, and the
publisher hereby disclaims any responsibility for them.

This is a work of fiction. All of the characters, names, incidents,
organizations, and dialogue in this novel are either the products of the
author's imagination or are used fictitiously.

ISBN: 978-0-595-52804-2 (pbk)
ISBN: 978-0-595-62858-2 (ebk)

Printed in the United States of America

This book is a gift to the worldwide family of Tehya. Please share it. One-half of the proceeds or royalties from sales of the book will be donated to those who are working to eliminate poverty and promote peace.

Contents

The Parable of Tehya is one continuous story. It does not take long to read. Please read the *Preface, Author's Note,* and the *Introduction* to set the stage. You will be ready to enjoy and to ponder the meaning of what Tehya sees, hears, feels, learns, and communicates along her way. It is possible that Tehya's childhood journey is, in some ways, similar to your own. Share this story with your children, grandchildren, and great grandchildren. They may find a kindred spirit in Tehya.

Dedication

This book is dedicated to your children, to your grandchildren, and to your great grandchildren...*and to mine.*

Acknowledgements

As the author, I wish to acknowledge all the angels who have met me at the crossroads of life to help me know I was on the path I was meant to take.

You, the Reader

Thank you for reading *The Parable of Tehya*. Please share the book with others to spread its message of hope and peace. Tell them where you obtained your copy.

Preface

This is a parable about *original beauty...tribes...*and *the importance of one child*.

When the water first springs from a mountainside, it glistens with purity. When the land awakens from winter, it is alive with sprouting seeds that turn the land to green. After a desert storm, tadpoles appear as if from nowhere. A newborn child is soft and tender. In all the origins of the world and the things in it, there is a fresh start and innocence. There is *original beauty*.

As we came to earth and explored our new home, we wandered from forest glens to fertile valleys. We searched for food. We found each other. We formed friendships. We multiplied. We made enemies. We fought. We formed *tribes* to reassure us and to protect us. This book is about such tribes.

We are all of tribal origins and our allegiance to "tribes" continues to this very day. We observe many rich traditions among our tribes and yet there is conflict.

Finally, this book is about *the importance of one child*. In this parable, the one child we will know best is Tehya. I use this name to honor the native people of my land, yet my intent is not that she represents any one tribe or people. She could be your ancestor—a young woman of *your tribe*. As you ponder the story and share it with others, you will see that Tehya is any child. She is each child into whose eyes you have looked as you wondered at the innocence, the vulnerability, and the original beauty of that child.

It is the nature of children to trust. They know only the tribal boundaries we adults teach them. And then they grow up. They become us. They inherit our fears, our hopes, and the effects of our mistakes as well as our achievements. While they are still young, they can teach us. They remind us of what we have forgotten as we sometimes wander from our own original beauty. Deep down, we yearn that each child has the opportunity to learn, to be safe, and to be loved.

An Author's Note for Further Understanding

To help you understand the world of Tehya and the meaning I have placed into it, I offer the following insights about the genesis and the construction of this parable.

This is a story of fear and love...of conflict and cooperation...of scarcity and abundance...of prejudice and peace. Some who read this book may think me to be overly idealistic. My response would be to ask what they would have me advocate. Would it be a "reasonable level of poverty" in the world or "justifiable hatred" or only a little war when it becomes necessary? Perhaps our track record as "civilized" societies has discouraged us from contemplating the ideal. As we strive to love the world we live in, we must continue to lift it higher as we do.

The images I have created in this book are a composite of wonderful things I have learned over the years, beautiful places I've been, and the impressions I have of marvelous people of both the past and the present in many cultures around the world. As you walk beside Tehya, you will mingle with her people and with those of neighboring villages. Learn from the people of each village—who they are and what they stand for.

The insights are not about *what* or *who* is *bad* or *good*. The insights are about moving beyond the unhelpful and unkind inclinations that are sometimes part of our human nature so that we may all bring our good gifts together to link our villages and to make the tribes of which we are a part more tolerant and more inclusive.

Tehya is an intelligent young woman in a simpler world than ours but with nevertheless complex issues of humanity and of the spirit. Perhaps in her simpler world, we can see these spiritual issues more clearly than amidst the clamor of a modern world.

Introduction

Tehya's story is set in a time long ago that seems like yesterday. It takes place in a far-away land that may remind you of a village nearby. The parable reveals ancient wisdom that is truth for a modern world.

The story is shared with the world at a time of great hope and great fear—a time when humans are more powerful than ever before and yet as vulnerable as they ever were.

Tehya is not merely a figment of imagination. *Who she would be* lives in those she represents from every corner of the world. In her, you may see you. Through her, you will see your children. In those who surround her, you will see your extended family, your neighbors, and those with whom you work each day. Through her, you will see leaders of nations and institutions of all kinds. You will share Tehya's yearning that these many people will come together in new ways.

The language of the story is a simplified form of a modern vernacular, yet you can imagine Tehya thinking and speaking in her native tongue.

The story begins just a short time before birth as Tehya (tĕh-yăh) watches her parents anticipate her arrival. She listens as her parents discuss her name and their hopes and their fears.

She is eager to rejoin these special friends in the new home they have prepared for her on earth.

Join Tehya now as she makes her entry. Share her thoughts and impressions. Think what she is thinking and feel what she is feeling. Listen to her first earthly observations…

Birth

"My mother is crying. She is hurting, yet she is happy. She is so anxious to see me. I've been waiting for this moment. There is pressure...cold...a sudden pulling and lifting. My cry is my greeting. I am the one you will call Tehya."

"It hurts," cries Tehya's mother as she raises her head, sweat dripping from her face, "Is the baby all right?"

"She is perfect. She is kicking already, she's kicking." Tehya's father has spoken for the first time since the birth process began.

Inside Tehya's mind there is now a sensation of swirling, of some thoughts being erased and replaced by new sounds and impressions. Next, she is in her father's arms and he sways from left to right. From his face comes a soft, muffled sound that is so comforting. Others have come into the room to admire Tehya and express their delight. Tehya's mother settles calmly into the furry blankets of her bed. She whispers to her husband, "Give her to me."

"Tehya, you are my precious one. I have loved you for many months. I am ready to feed you. Come closer now. Shhh, all of you. I am happy you are happy for us. Now it's time to speak softly so Tehya can eat and then sleep."

Family and friends move to the outer room and continue their chatter and their hugging. Tehya's mother is momentarily closer to heaven—the heaven Tehya just left. A new world is what Tehya faces. Her parents' world has been altered forever. As old friends, they are now reunited in the new earthly roles of child and mother and father.

This is the story of Teyha. Her fears, her dreams, and her hopes may resonate with your own and with those of so many others in the wide world around us. She will speak to us with simplicity and remind us of things we may already

1

know in our hearts. Enjoy her story as she grows up, as she awakens to the original beauty of her new world, and as she makes the difference she was meant to make in her time and in ours.

Growing Up / Watching

Tehya awoke from her nap. Her eyes tingled. She wiped the sleepy dust from the corner of each eye as she sat up. It was cold. She pulled her blanket over her shoulders and looked outside. Would the trees soon be green again, she wondered? A dog barked and she jumped. It was not her puppy. It belonged to Akule who lived at the end of the village. She saw Akule come running. He pulled the door to Tehya's house open and shouted, "Hurry, the antelope are crossing the river. There is a very large herd. The men have gone to hunt."

Tehya's mother heard Akule. "Tehya," she said. "You cannot go with Akule. There are too many antelope. They cannot see small children in the grass and will run over you. Let the men hunt. Akule, please wait. I will bring Tehya and we will go up the hill to watch the antelope and the hunters."

Tehya's mother took Akule's dog to its home and she and the two children started up the hill. Small rabbits jumped from behind the sagebrush as they walked. They were delighted to see early spring flowers—blue, yellow, and Tehya's favorite red flowers. She was so happy to have a mother and a friend.

The air was cold, but the sun was shining. When they reached the top of the hill, they could see the river and the prairie stretching into the distance—no antelope and no hunters. Suddenly, a hawk swooped down, not far from them. Its claws opened as it snatched a small mouse that had just climbed to the top of its burrow. With a great swish, the bird flew away with its catch.

Tehya was so impressed by the flapping wings of the hawk but sad for the mouse. She turned to her mother with much seriousness and said, "Mother, the world is about hunting and eating, isn't it?"

"Not only hunting and eating, my dear child. It is also about building a home and making a place for your babies."

3

"But what if the mother has her babies and the hawk eats the mother?"

"Dear child, the mouse built a safe home. The babies are safe. The father will bring them food. They will grow up. The hawk must eat, but he will catch only some of the mice. Others will eat many seeds, have their babies, and grow old without being eaten."

Tehya thought to herself how wise her mother was. She hoped she would never be killed and eaten like the mouse. "Mother, is daddy like the hawk hunting antelope?"

"Yes, daughter, the winter is still here. We must have meat until the corn and the berries come and we catch more fish. Then, your father will not need to kill so many antelope."

"Is father brave?"

"Yes, he is very brave. He must be strong to run after the antelope and to carry one home to us."

Mother's Hands

As night came, Tehya's mother cooked. Then, it was time to sleep.

Mother placed her hands on Tehya's cheeks. "Child, you are like a sunbeam to me. You make my life bright. You make me very happy. Now, go to sleep, so your sunbeam will become stronger and light up the room in the morning when you awake." Tehya's mother stroked her daughter's silky black hair. Tehya thought to herself how soft her mother's hands were. These hands made her feel very safe. She had seen her mother gently pick a flower and hold it carefully in front of her face and smile. These hands made Tehya feel like a beautiful flower.

Tehya's older brother, Hakan, had lain down on the other side of the room. He made the sound of a moose. It was not a very good imitation, but Tehya knew he was just trying to make her angry. She laughed and said, "Go to sleep, moose."

Father's Hands

Morning came. There was loud noise outside. Dogs barking. Men yelling. Children laughing. "The men are back. They have many antelope."

Tehya watched as the men came near. They did not walk into the village. They walked behind the houses to a row of trees where the antelope would be skinned and cut into pieces. Some antelope meat would be eaten very soon. Other meat would be left hanging to dry and used another day.

Tehya asked her mother if she could go and watch the men. She ran to the trees where the men were working. Her father turned and saw her. He smiled and shouted, "Children, watch us, but stay back. Stand over there and watch."

Tehya did watch as her father lifted a large antelope easily into the tree and tied it to a branch. He was so strong. His hands moved swiftly holding the knives needed to cut the antelope's skin from the meat. These hands with the knives seemed to Tehya very much like the claws of the hawk she had seen yesterday. Her father had much skill. The skin of the antelope would be quickly and cleanly removed and then rubbed and dried to become clothing for her and Hakan.

There was a small trickle of water coming from the rocks near the antelope skinning place. As the men finished, they washed their hands. Tehya's father came toward her. He reached out and picked her up just like the antelope. He held her high over his head and laughed. "You are so beautiful, little daughter." His hands were large. She felt as if she were being held in the branches of a great tree. Then, he put her gently on the ground. She was dizzy and began to stumble. Father reached out and grabbed her arm to pull her up. He said, "Be careful. Watch where you are walking or you will trip on the rocks." His voice was also strong. She knew she should do as he said.

Sunshine, Darkness, and Rain

As the spring came, Tehya noticed how the wild flowers spread across the meadow and through the forest. As she arose and went outside each morning, she loved to walk through the new grass with its thin layer of frost. She enjoyed the soft "crunch, crunch" sound as she walked. The sunshine would peek through the trees and light up the flowers. The way the flowers opened their petals reminded Tehya of how she rubbed her sleepy eyes when she awoke.

Afternoon would often bring large, billowy clouds rolling across the small lake where her people fished and where she and Hakan and their friends swam and played. First the clouds were beautiful and white. They would swell like the white kernels of corn her mother would soak in water and then roast on the round stone she placed in the cooking fire. Gradually the clouds would become angry and dark. She knew rain would come. Sometimes it fell softly. Sometimes it brought a flood that caused her father to worry about their house. Once the water washed through the village and over the mounds of dirt her father had placed to guard their home. The rain came inside the house and made her blankets wet. She was very cold that night.

Tehya's father explained that the coming of light and darkness and rain were God's way of making the earth churn the same way mother stirred the ground corn together with salt and savory plant leaves and water to make the cakes that were Tehya's favorite food. "God must make a great cake," her father would say. "God mixes water with earth and with seeds to make the cake. The sunshine cooks it. Then bushes grow berries and trees grow nuts. The antelope eat these and the grass. The antelope are also our food. This is the way God makes the earth work for us."

Tehya loved to eat, just like the antelope that ate the berries and nuts and chewed the grass. She loved the antelope, too.

7

Trees

Tehya had a favorite tree. She would stand beneath it and wonder how it grew so tall. When the rain came, its branches would catch the water and keep her dry. She felt safe near the trunk of this forest friend.   Her father cut smaller trees to make their house. Old trees were cut down to make the fire that she would sit and watch, which gave light to the nighttime and let her mother cook so many things. Fire and wood: she knew these were magical and so important.

One day, a few months ago, Tehya and Akule were playing among the small trees near the water spring. They took a knife and made their marks on the bark of two trees. They planned to make walking poles like the elders in the village used. They tried to bend the trees, but these were too young and too strong to break. Their knives were too small to cut the trees down. So, they cut many circles in the bark and peeled rings of bark from the trees to decorate them instead. They thought their tree bark designs were beautiful.

Father came to find them for dinner. When he saw the trees, he was very angry. He told Hakan and Tehya that the young trees would now die and it would take as many years as they were old for new trees to grow in their place. He told them to care for the trees as if they were friends. Tehya asked, "Father, you cut trees. Does it hurt them?" Father replied, "Tehya, we cut only trees to make shelter or we cut old trees for firewood. Do you know that we travel far from the village to cut these trees and we move from place to place to cut only some trees, then we move on?"

"Yes, father. Why?"

"This is because we cannot cut too many trees in one place. If we do, the rain will wash the earth away. The tree roots hold the earth together. We only cut some trees among other trees. If there are too many tall trees covering the sky, the smaller trees cannot see the sunshine. We cut the old trees for firewood. If the old trees are gone and the lightning comes, the forest will not burn so easily. We plant new trees where there are not enough. God has given us the trees. They are our friends. God expects us to care for them and they will help us make our houses. They will help us stay warm and cook our food."

"Father, who made the world?"

"Tehya, a Great Spirit made this world."

"Who is the Great Spirit, father?"

"This spirit is the one I call God."

"Why did God make the world?"

"Daughter, do you know the shiny stone that hangs from your mother's neck?"

"Of course, father. Mother promised to give it to me when I find my husband. I don't want to wait. I want a shiny stone around my neck now. Will you find me one?"

"No, Tehya, you will love the stone your mother will give you even more, I promise you. Be patient. You will grow up soon enough and there will be a husband for you."

"But you did not answer my question. Why did God make the world?"

"Tehya, I cut and polished the stone to hang around your mother's neck to show my love for her and to help her feel even more beautiful. God made the world to hang in the sky, to shine in the blackness, and to make the sky more beautiful. God made the world to show love for us. The Great Spirit made a home for us as I have made a home for you."

Tehya smiled. She loved her father. She loved God. Both had made beautiful homes for her.

Howling and Fear

When the wolves howled at night, Tehya was so glad her mother and father were nearby. Her friends had told her that wolves would come and take children by the leg in their teeth and drag them away into the woods and eat them. Father told Tehya this was not true. The wolves were howling to speak to their friends—to their pack. He explained that wolves were frightened of humans and looking for antelope just like the humans. Perhaps they were jealous that we took their food. Tehya thought about the wolves. It is true that she had never had one of her friends taken by wolves.

"Father, what is a pack?" Tehya asked.

"A pack is a village of wolves. They stay together as we stay together with those in our village."

"I thought a village was a place with homes. Do the wolves have homes?"

"Yes, sometimes they live in burrows and sometimes in caves. These are safe places for their cubs and away from the rain and snow, just like our homes."

"Why do we and the wolves stay in packs and villages, father?"

"When there are many, it is easier to hunt the antelope. When people live in villages they can do different things for each other. Some members of our village do one thing best. Others do something else better. You know the round stone your mother uses to cook in the fire. This stone was made by Chesmu. He enjoys working with stones. He does not like to hunt. And you know Kasa. She is your mother's friend and made your blankets. She sews many things for us that we do not sew for ourselves: coats, blankets, and even the cloth sacks for the antelope meat. In our village we work together to get many things done."

"Is that all, father?"

"No, Tehya. Those in our village come from the same families who have lived in this land for many years. We know the same ways. We have the same faces. We like to look at these faces that we know and trust. These people are of our own tribe."

"Father, when you call us 'tribe,' is this the same as 'village' or 'pack'? What do you mean when you say 'our tribe'?"

"Our tribe means 'our people,' Tehya—our people."

"The other children tell me there are other tribes. Where are they?"

"The other tribes live in faraway places. They have their own places. Some live in the valleys. Some live in the mountains. They must stay in their places."

"Why, father?"

"Because, they will be safe there and we will be safe here."

"Are we afraid of the others? Can we go see them?"

"No. Yes. Tehya, I mean, no, we are not afraid and, no, we cannot go see them."

"Why, father?"

"They are too far away. They are too busy. And the antelope that cross the river are our antelope and they must not kill our antelope. Your mother will also tell you that we do not have enough nuts and corn for two tribes. The other tribes must find their own food."

"So, father, we are afraid that if they come to our village, they will steal our food. I don't want them to come. I am afraid. Are their faces different? Will their faces frighten me? I think we have our tribe to protect us from the other tribes. Is this true, father?"

"Child, you ask too many questions. Go help your mother. It is time for the planting of corn and we must all help."

The Corn Planting

Tehya was happy it was time to plant the corn. She enjoyed digging in the dirt with her corn stick. Her mother trusted her to place the seed corn into the ground. She was excited because it would soon be time for the corn planting celebration. All of the families of the village would gather in the meadow for singing and dancing and for prayers.

Akule's father was the Spirit Man for Tehya's tribe. He would speak the prayers for the tribe. The mother of her good friend, Mansi, would bring the drums and music sticks and give these to members of the tribe to make the cheerful sounds that helped the dancers dance. Tehya would dance with her friends. There was a large circle of stones in the meadow. The men had built a huge fire inside the circle and the people of the village began to gather. The fire had fingers that reached up to the stars as if to touch them. Tehya thought that the stars might be sparks that flew up to heaven long ago and were stuck on the roof of the sky. Perhaps these ancient sparks in the sky called out to people on earth to build fires and to try to reach heaven. Fire was magic. The stars were magic. These made Tehya think of God who made them all. There is something bigger than planting corn, sewing blankets, and hunting antelope, she imagined. What could be so big? What did God do all day?

The music began. Many busy feet shuffled in the dirt around the fire circle. There was dust and smoke. There was chanting and singing. Tehya danced with Mansi and with Akule. Akule made faces at her. He stuck out his tongue and licked his face. She pushed him away. The families of the village were so happy. Tehya liked to call these people she loved, "her village," and not a tribe. She did not like the word, "tribe."

Akule's father now stood very close to the fire. He raised his hands and then lowered them. He raised them again and lowered them. Everybody around the fire stopped dancing and grew quiet. The Spirit Man raised his arms again and prayed.

"Oh, Great Spirit, we love our village. We love you. We love the trees and the bushes and their fruit. We love the many antelope you have sent to us. We love the sky. As we plant our corn, we ask that the sky will open to bring rain so the corn will grow. We ask that we will have peace in our village. We have had many years of peace. We pray that other tribes will have peace in their faraway places and not come to our village. Great Spirit, who we call God, smile upon us. We will do good. We will love our families. We will be strong."

The Spirit Man then stomped his feet and gave a loud yell. He said, "Dance more. Dance to please God."

The dancing began again. This time, there was yelling and laughing. This was fun. Tehya knew that bedtime would come too soon. She wished to dance all night.

Suddenly, from across the meadow, a young man came running and shouting. "Come quick. Someone has been in our village. I saw them. They were in the house with the seed corn. Some sacks of corn are gone. I saw their eyes in the dark and I frightened them away."

Tehya's father now spoke, but just five short words, spoken more loudly than she had ever heard her father speak, "Be quiet all of you." Then he said, "Mothers, keep your children by the fire. Men, make a circle around me, now."

Tehya stood back, near the fire with her mother. She could not hear what the men were saying, but they were angry. They raised their fists in the air and stomped their feet. She could see the shoulders of the young men in the firelight. They were very strong. She was frightened, more than when the wolves howled.

The Plan

Tehya's father was a very wise man. The other men wanted to chase the robbers of the seed corn into the night. They looked to Tehya's father and shouted their angry intent, "We will get our spears and leave now. If these men from another tribe are nearby, we will find them. If not, we will follow their trail to know which tribe it is that has come into our homeland to threaten our corn crop and our families. We must show them that we are strong and have many sharp spears. We must frighten them. If they do not listen, we will kill them."

Tehya's father spoke, "It is possible that these men are hungry and do not have seed corn to plant for their families. Perhaps a few sacks of seed corn are all they need. We have much seed corn from the rich harvest last year and God will bless us with another good harvest this year, which will feed our people. We should wait for summer. If these men do not come again soon, they do not plan to steal from us again and their tribe will not make war upon us. Let us wait. If the men do come, we will know they want to harm to us and our children would go hungry. Then, we will make war on their tribe to stop them."

The angry men listened. They became quiet and lowered their fists. They agreed: "We must wait for a season—until summer comes, to see if these men will do no more harm to our village."

When Tehya's father returned home, Tehya pretended to be asleep, but she was so eager to know what the men planned to do. "Father, will the men go hunting for the others?"

"No, my daughter, the men will wait. The men who came to our village and stole from us did not burn the corn house or hurt our people. Perhaps they are hungry. We will wait to see if they come to trouble us again."

"What did they look like, father?"

"Tehya, I did not see them. It was too dark to know the tribe of these men."

"How do you know which tribe they belong to?"

"Sometimes they wear their own color around their waists or across their shoulders. Sometimes, they carry different spears that we recognize. And, sometimes their skin is the color of the antelope's back."

"Father, they have different skin?"

"No, it is skin like ours, but a different color."

"What does this mean?"

"It means their families are from the valleys faraway, that is all it means."

"Father, what is the color of our tribe that we must wear?"

"Tehya, it is the color of the grass that you now wear around your shoulders. You knew that. Your mother has told you. This is why our women wear this green color more than any other color. It is our color--green. Go to sleep now."

Mother with Father

Tehya could not sleep. She heard her father speaking softly to her mother. She had been told that mothers and fathers must sleep on the other side of the wall, away from the children's sleeping place so they can talk alone at night to prepare for the new day—to know what will be best for their children. Tonight, Tehya was too curious. She slipped out of her blankets and crawled to the edge of the wall. As she looked across the room, she could see her mother's back. Her shoulders were bare and her hair was untied. She could see father's hand stroking mother's hair just like mother stroked her hair. She heard her mother softly say, "I am afraid for the children. Will the robbers come again?"

Tehya's father spoke softly, "My dear wife, you should not be afraid. I am here. I will protect our family. You know that. I love you. Come closer. I love you."

Tehya knew she should not watch her parents. This was their time. She crawled back to her blankets. She smiled. Her father did not say the word "love" often. This was the word mothers used when speaking to their children. It was the kindest word spoken by people of her village. They spoke of love for children and love of God, but the men and women did not often speak of love for each other. Perhaps they did this only at night when the children were sleeping. Tehya was so happy that her father loved her mother. She felt so safe now. Her father would protect her. Her mother would care for her. Her father and mother would do this together because they loved each other. Still, she was curious. Why were her mother's shoulders bare? It was still cold at night and she needed a blanket. Then, she understood. Father would keep her mother warm and happy tonight.

No More Robbers

The summer came. There were no more robbers. The corn was growing tall, but not all the corn. Some cornfields had much corn. Other cornfields did not. Tehya's father explained. Some of the seed corn that had been stored behind the bags that were stolen was older. It had been placed near the wall of the corn house where rain had come in and made it wet. This seed did not grow well. It would mean that there would be some very healthy corn, but perhaps not enough corn to feed the village through the winter and into the spring of the new year.

Mother's New Smile

Tehya began to notice that her mother was singing more while she worked. She would smile and sing softly and sometimes move her body from side to side with the sound of her music.

"Mother, are you more happy now that it is the end of summer?"

"No, child."

"Are you happy because I work so hard to help you?"

Tehya's mother laughed. "No, that's not the reason."

"Why are you so happy, Mother?"

"Come here, Tehya, and kneel down at my side." Tehya's mother pulled her dress up from one side, over her leg so Tehya could see her belly. It was swollen. Tehya knew from seeing many women with babies inside that her mother was pregnant. She giggled and said, "Mother, will I have a new brother or sister? Does father know about the baby?"

"Yes, Tehya, your father knows. He loved me to make the baby come into our home. We do not know if this baby will be a boy or a girl, yet. Perhaps in the fall, I will know and I will tell you. You and Hakan must help me and your father love this baby and protect it."

At first, Tehya could not speak. She just smiled and placed her head on her mother's lap. She wondered if she could hear the baby. Perhaps the baby would be singing the same song her mother sang. Tehya sat next to her mother for a long time. Finally, she had to ask, "Do babies sing before they are born, when they are inside their mothers? Do they learn songs in heaven?"

"Tehya, I think unborn babies do sing and sometimes they cry. I think they learn the songs from us—from their families."

"I am happy for you, Mother. Our new baby will have a good family."

Did God Forget?

Tehya went to visit her friend, Mansi. She found her friend sitting in the dirt drawing animal shapes with a stick. Mansi stopped. "Tehya, let's go to the water spring. I am thirsty."

"Let's go," said Tehya as she turned and began to run from the village. They raced to the spring and arrived together, laughing, and happy to be friends.

"Where does the water come from, Tehya? Is it from God?"

"I don't know. I think it is from the snow in the mountains. Mansi, God doesn't take care of everything, you know."

"What do you mean?"

"Do you remember when the Spirit Man prayed for rain so the corn would grow?"

"Yes."

"We had some rain, but not plenty of rain, my father told me. And, some of the corn did not grow. Maybe God forgot to take care of our corn."

"Tehya, I don't know. Let's go and ask my mother."

The two girls took their drink from the spring and ran back to Mansi's house.

"Mother, Mother," began Mansi. "Why did God forget to send more rain? Why did God forget to take care of our corn?"

"Wait, my child. God does not forget. The Great Spirit knows we are here and cares for us, but God does not change the wind and move the clouds just for us. These move in their own way. Sometimes God will choose to send a miracle. Sometimes God will choose to let us learn from the good harvests and the poor harvests. When there is not so much rain and some of the corn does not grow, we learn to eat more carefully and to not waste the corn we have. We learn to store more corn for the years of poor harvest. You see, some of God's children are also praying for not too much rain. They have had floods with too much rain. God hears all prayers, but only changes the world for a miracle, now and then. The best prayer to God is a prayer to be wise and to know how to learn from the world and to do our best to live in the world. This time is our time for learning."

"Thank you, Mother."

Tehya and Mansi went back outside and raced again to the other end of the village. "Goodbye, Mansi. Your mother is wise like my mother. God did not forget us."

Angry Parents

As Tehya walked to the door of her house, she heard loud voices. Father was angry and speaking very loudly to her mother. She heard him say, "You let Hakan use my tools. He has lost my favorite knife somewhere in the forest. You were foolish to let him take it from the house." Tehya peeked inside the door. Her mother was crying. Then she spoke loudly to father, "You should be here to help your son. You are always with the other men hunting or making your spears. I think you and the other men think too much of war. We need you here at home."

Tehya's father turned and walked quickly through the door nearly trampling Tehya under his feet. As he did, he said, "Move child. Get out my way."

Sometimes Tehya had seen her parents angry. This made her very sad and frightened that she would not have a home if they were angry too much.

Tehya's mother saw her outside the door. "Tehya, come here, please. Child, you look so worried."

"Mother, I thought father loved you. He spoke so angrily to you. Why?"

"He feels many pressures. He is the chief of the warriors who must protect our village. He does not want to make war with the other tribes, but the other men tell him he must be prepared for war. This makes him angry and then he comes home to me and lets his anger out. Tonight, he will apologize to me. We do love each other. I am sorry that I spoke angrily back to him. Tehya, life is full of happiness and also full of work and sometimes worries. What we must all do is be patient when we can and learn to solve our problems when they come. Your father and I do solve problems well. He is a fine man. And, I should not have let your brother take father's favorite knife out of the house. Father was too angry. And I made a mistake. We will both learn."

"Mother, I am growing up, aren't I? I understand grown-up things, don't I?"

"Yes, you do."

Not Enough

The fall came and the leaves in the forest began to turn to many beautiful colors. Tehya loved the fall because the sky was very blue. The daytime was not so hot. Her blankets felt very good at night. Tehya remembered the stories of the special food her grandmother would prepare at the end of the harvest in the fall. Grandmother taught this special way to cook to Tehya's mother. Early each summer, the families of the village would plant a special garden for large orange and yellow squash. Then, in the fall, Grandmother would roast these squash and make special cakes with them.

Tehya missed her grandmother. She remembered that she had become very old with many wrinkles. Tehya was so young then. She could not remember much more, just squash cakes and the wrinkles on her grandmother's face. Her grandfather died three years before she was born. He had gone for a long hunt in early winter and became lost. He died because he could not find his way home and became frozen somewhere in the forest. The people of the village never found him. This was the story of her grandparents.

As the fall came, the people of the village met to discuss the supply of food for winter. They decided there were not enough of corn and nuts and other food to get them through the winter. More hunting and fishing would be needed. Some snow had already fallen in the mountains. The men would go as Tehya's grandfather did to find the great elk herd or perhaps bears before their winter hibernation began. The bears would be fat from eating so many berries.

Tehya's father told his family about the shortage of food and the need for a long hunt. Tehya and Hakan were worried. "Mother, father, will we be hungry this winter?"

"Children, if we are a little hungry, it will be good for us. We will not be fat like the bears. Then, we can run even faster."

"Will we eat the bears," Hakan asked?

"I do not like the bear's meat," said Tehya.

"Children, you will be happy to have meat this winter. And we will be careful with the sacks of corn and nuts that we have stored for the winter. We will be wise and strong until the spring comes again."

The Hunting

The men began to prepare for the big hunt. Tehya enjoyed watching the men prepare for a hunt. They worked hard. They were so busy. And, their faces had special wrinkles and no smiles until one of the men would throw something at another man. They would wrestle and laugh. Then, they would be busy again. Men like to wrestle and pretend to fight. Her father said this was to help them practice for war if they needed to protect the village.

Once, Tehya asked her father, "Why don't the women wrestle? I know they don't make wars, but, if wrestling is fun, women would like it, too. Why don't they wrestle?"

Father replied, "Tehya, there are two reasons women do not wrestle. The first reason is that this is not their way. They are women. The second reason is that women are more kind than men. Sometimes they are too kind. They would not make good warriors. They would talk to the enemy of friendship and be killed. They do not understand this."

That night, Tehya noticed that father and mother were sleeping very close to each other. They were showing their love because father would be away for many days and father did not want mother to be lonely. Tehya understood. She hoped she would have a husband like her father who would love her in such a gentle way.

The next morning, Tehya stood with Hakan and with Akule and Mansi as the men put water, food, leather ropes, and spears on their backs. They were ready. Father came to the children and kneeled down beside them. He said, "Stay with your mother. Obey her. We will soon return with food for the village. I love you." Tehya's father quickly turned his head away, stood up, and joined the other men.

Tehya knew that the men would walk over many hills and through valleys until they found the elk and the bear. Nothing would stop them. She knew they would return with meat.

The Gathering

That afternoon, mother asked the children to come inside. She said, "Children, while the men are away, we need to make a special gathering of any corn that is lying in the fields. We must go to the forest and search for nuts. And there are still some bushes with berries. We will collect these and dry these. We will put these in the sacks at the corn house. All this food we gather and store will help us through the winter. Come with me. Take these sacks and we will go to the fields and to the forest."

As they walked into the forest, they followed the path the men had taken earlier that morning. Tehya noticed that some of the bushes with berries had been trampled under the men's feet and smashed berries were visible in the dirt. "Mother, why did the men walk on the berries?"

"They were in a hurry to find the elk."

"They should be more careful. We should have gathered the berries before they left."

"Tehya, the men do not see the berries. They look straight ahead. Nothing will stop them until they find the elk and the bear."

"I am glad you and I see the berries."

"Yes, there must be berries and nuts and corn and meat. It is good that the men know how to find the meat."

"Mother, could we find meat, too? Could you and I hunt elk and bear? Is this something only men can do?"

"No, not just men hunt. Women can hunt. I have seen women kill antelope. If there were no men, I would hunt, but men have bigger shoulders to carry the antelope and elk and bear meat home to us. I am happy to let them hunt."

"Can men pick berries and corn?"

"Yes, you know this. You have picked the corn with your father. You forgot. Men like the berries and will pick them when they are hungry. What I have noticed about men is that they pick the berries too fast and, remember, they don't see all the berries. They are thinking about other things when they pick berries. When I pick berries I mostly think about you and Hakan eating the berries and smiling."

The Others

Akule and Tehya sat outside in the cool fall evening. They did not want to go inside. There were so many stars. Tehya told Akule about the men and the berries. He laughed and said, "I only pick berries when I'm hungry. I would rather hunt antelope. Hunting is for men. I am a man—almost. I am already brave. I have killed rattlesnakes. Tehya, you are brave, too. I think we are both growing up. Our parents need our help. I think we should learn about the other tribes— the tribes of those men who came to steal our seed corn. Tomorrow, while our mothers are busy, we can run over the hill to the north to find their village."

"No, Akule, our parents have told us it is forbidden to go to that place. My father told me there are many bears living on the hill and we should not go there."

"I promise we will watch for bears. If there are any bears at all, we will turn around and run home. But, I don't understand. If there are so many bears on that hill, why didn't the men go there to hunt? Maybe over that hill is where the other tribes live. We can go quietly through the forest and see for ourselves."

"No, Akule. This is too dangerous…but, I do want to see their faces. Father says their faces are different and their skin is the color of the antelope's back."

"Tomorrow we will decide."

"I must go home, Akule."

Early the next morning, Akule knocked on the side of Tehya's house where he knew she slept. Tehya was startled but guessed that the knock was Akule. She dressed. She took a small sack with nuts from the shelf near the door and went outside.

"Let's go," said Akule.

"Alright, but what if our mothers are worried?"

"They will think we are playing at the water spring. We will be back before they worry too much."

The children went quietly around the back of the house and then walked briskly yet carefully to get away from the village without disturbing their families. As they came to the meadow, they ran faster. Soon they were at the edge of the forest that covered the north hill. Tehya said, "Akule, we must rest."

They sat down. They ate some of the nuts in Tehya's sack. Akule had a leather flask with water. They both drank and were ready to go up the hill. Rather than go straight up the hill, they went around the side of the hill and wound their way to the ridge near the top of the hill where they knew they could see the other side.

The children came to top of the ridge and sat down. They were exhausted and took another drink from Akule's flask. "Look, Tehya. Look. There are houses, there to the left, at the bottom of the hill, over there." Akule pointed with his right hand as he touched Tehya's cheek with the other hand to turn her face in the proper direction.

The children walked carefully through the forest on this strange new side of the north hill. They came nearer and nearer to the other tribe's village. Some people were outside working. Children were playing. Tehya and Akule knew they should not go much closer. As they watched, the people looked the same as their own people, from a distance. The children made familiar sounds as they danced about and played. The houses were similar, but were not made of so many sticks. There were animal hides between the sticks for walls. It looked like these houses could blow away in a strong wind.

"Akule, we must go."

"You're right. Let's go back now before they see us."

Just as the children turned to go home, a stone came rolling down the hill. They were startled. As they looked up, they saw a young boy scurry behind some small trees. Akule ran toward him. The boy fell. Akule knew the boy was smaller and he knew he could wrestle him. As he came closer, the younger boy laid down on his face with his arms wrapped around his head. This was the position Akule's father had taught him if a bear should come. His father told him, if a bear comes and there is no tree to climb, he should lie down and pretend to be dead with his arms around his head to protect his face from the bear's claws. Akule knew the younger boy thought Akule would kill him. He stopped and spoke softly, "Don't be afraid. I won't hurt you." Then, Tehya spoke softly, "Hello, don't run away."

The boy slowly lifted his head. As Akule and Tehya spoke, he shook his head. He said some words that Akule and Tehya did not understand. The two of them carefully approached the boy. Tehya showed her bag of nuts and reached in to collect a handful. As soon as the boy saw the nuts, his eyes lit up and he reached out. He scraped the nuts from Tehya's hand and caught one that nearly fell to the ground. He ate the nuts very quickly and smiled. Then he ran off through the woods. For such a cool fall day, he did not have many clothes. His arms and legs were very thin.

Tehya and Akule now ran straight up the hill, into the woods, and over the ridge. By the time they got back to their village, the sun was directly above them in the sky. They knew it was midday. They had been gone too long. There were many women standing at the edge of the village. As they expected, both of their mothers were among them and came running as soon as they saw their children. Tehya's mother smiled and cried. Akule's mother scolded them. "Where have you been, she asked? Did you go over the north hill? There are bears there."

The two children were quiet and shook their heads. The women and children walked toward their homes. When they came to Akule's house, both mothers insisted the children

31

come inside. "Children, where did you go? What did you see? Why did you disobey us?" Parents ask so many questions.

Tehya spoke. "We went to the other side of the hill. We saw another village. Mother, the people are the same. They work. Their children were playing. Their houses are not strong. We think the wind will blow them away."

"Did you go into the village?

"No, we were afraid and stopped in the forest at the edge of their village and watched."

"Did you speak to anyone or just look from far away."

Akule slid his foot against Tehya's and gently shook his head to signal, "No." Tehya looked at her mother and said, "No, mother. We did not speak to anyone."

Hakan's Happiness

Tehya had just finished lunch when she heard the other children screaming. "They're home. They're home." The men were returning from the hunt. She was so excited. She jumped up, grabbed her mother's hand and said, "Let's go. Come with me. Let's go."

Tehya and her mother went outside just in time to see father holding his spear high above his head as he approached the house and smiled at them. Father was helping the other men carry large animal carcasses on poles that rested on their shoulders. "What a heavy load," Tehya thought to herself. "I could not carry such a heavy animal all the way from the mountains."

Father nodded to Tehya and her mother. He and his friend who was helping to carry the dead animal went behind the house and placed the two poles on a special frame used for drying meat. He then returned to the door where Tehya and her mother were standing. He looked down at mother's belly. "My wife, your belly is bigger. The baby will come soon. Your face is so beautiful. With the baby inside you, your cheeks have turned red and shine like the early morning sun. I am glad you are well. Tehya, come here." He hugged his daughter. Then he hugged his wife.

Hakan came running. "Father, Father, you're home. I found your knife. It isn't lost."

"Hakan, you are becoming a man. Soon you will have a knife like mine."

"And a spear like yours, too, father?"

"Not for 4 or 5 years, Hakan. Not yet. Be patient."

Father was very tired. Mother fixed him lunch. The children sat and watched while he ate. They were proud of him and let him enjoy his food.

"Father," said Hakan, "Did you kill elk and bear? What is in the sacks? Is it bear meat or elk?"

"Son, there are six elk and two bears. We had a good hunt. We will go again to get more elk, but the bears will be hibernating. So, no more bears."

"I saw the elks' antlers. Did you bring the bears' heads and claws? I want to have one of the bear's claws, father."

Father smiled and said nothing.

"Father, come on, are there bear claws?"

"Son, there are enough bear claws and elk antlers for each boy in the village. Because I was one of the leaders of the hunt, the men let me choose the best of the bear claws for you."

Father reached in his pocket and pulled out a small folded piece of leather. Inside was a large bear claw.

"Oh, great God, thank you. It is wonderful."

"Hakan, be careful how you use God's name."

"But, father, he made the bear and helped you find it. I am thanking him."

"I understand, my son. So you know, this claw is not only big, but look closely. It is nearly perfect. It is not broken as some claws are. We will make a hole in the large end of the claw so you can hang it from a leather string and wear it around your neck."

A boy was never happier; a father was never more tired.

The Truth

Father went to the side of the room where he and mother slept. He lay down and mother lay down beside him. They both went to sleep. Tehya and Hakan went outside to play. Hakan had a splendid prize to show his friends. He ran to the other boys. One of the hunters was displaying a bear's head that had been carried home to the village in a sack. The boys were excited and exchanging stories their fathers had already told them. Some boys had bear claws. Some had elk horn.

Tehya stayed back and sat on a smooth rock near their house. She had a heavy heart because she knew she had told an untruth to her mother. With father back, she knew she could not hide the truth any longer. She must tell them when they awoke from their nap. While she waited, she walked slowly by herself to the water spring. This was her favorite place. The sound of the water trickling over the rocks was very peaceful. It took Tehya's worries away as it flowed along. The water coming from the rocks had slowed down after the long, hot summer. Soon there would be snow in the mountains and the cold air would make the water freeze. By the water spring, there was a small pool and around it there was usually a plant growing that Tehya especially liked to eat. The children called it the water leaf. It was sweet and bitter. Sometimes she would bring salt in her pocket. She would put salt in one hand and rub the green leaves in it. This was a favorite food. But the plant was gone now.

Tehya sat down by the spring. Her mind wandered. She thought how exciting it would be when her new brother or sister came. Mother told her she believed the baby was a girl. Perhaps she would have a sister now and a brother, Hakan. This was her wish. Tehya was also worried about the tribe that lived on the other side of the north hill. Would they be friends or would the men of her village make a war with them?

The truth she must tell her parents would make a difference. She began to think more seriously of what she would say to them.

Tehya walked back to her house. She saw her mother standing in the door looking from left to right, probably wondering where to find her daughter.

"Mother, here I am."

"Good. Please come in. Father wants to talk with you."

Tehya was worried. Did her father know? She entered the house.

Right away, father said, "Tehya, sit down. Please tell me all the things you and Hakan and your friends did while I was away. Did you help your mother?"

"Father, we played and we helped Mother. We talked of you often. I was worried that you might get lost in the snow and freeze like grandfather. I am so happy you are home. Thank you for bringing us meat. Did Mother show you the extra corn and nuts and berries we found?"

"Child, you and your mother did well. With the extra corn, nuts, berries, and meat, we will have enough for the winter—not plenty, but enough."

"Father, why do we have enough and others do not?"

"What do you mean, Tehya? The families in our village share. There are no families that will go hungry. Our village will have enough."

"What about the other villages—the other tribes, father? Will they have enough?"

"I hope they do. They must worry about this and gather food and find meat as we do."

"Father, what if their hunters are not successful? What if their spears are not as good as your spear, father? What if the rain did not come to their village and they have no corn?"

"Tehya, this is not your worry. Why are you thinking of this? This is for grown-ups to think about."

"Father, I saw a boy. Akule and I saw a boy."

"What boy? Where?"

"He was on the other side of the north hill and he was very hungry."

Tehya's mother was alarmed. "Tehya! Tehya! You said nothing of a boy. Father, Tehya and Akule disobeyed us. They went to the hill and over the ridge where the other tribe lives. They saw their village but did not go near it. I scolded them and knew we must talk about this soon. But, Tehya, you said nothing about a boy. What happened? Tell us now!"

Father sat quietly. Tehya knew he was angry and worried. She knew that some fathers would hit their children when the children disobeyed. Her father had never hit her and she was praying secretly that he would forgive her now. No one spoke.

It seemed like a long time that they waited. Then, Tehya's father spoke softly. "Daughter, I know children are curious. You and Akule are growing up. We cannot hide the truth about the other tribes from you any longer. Mother and I do not talk about the other tribes because we do not understand them. Once, when I met a man from that tribe on the north hill, he spoke to me with strange words I could not understand. When I spoke to him, he became frightened and ran away. We do not know their families. We do not know what they believe. We do not know how they live. We must live our way and let them live their way."

"Father, the boy spoke to us. We could not understand him. I showed him the nuts I brought in a sack. I held some in my hand. He smiled at me, took the nuts and quickly ate them. Then he ran away. Father, he did not have enough clothes for a cold winter. His legs and arms are very thin. I don't think his village will have enough for winter."

"Tehya, I am glad you have told us the truth. And now I have told you the truth about the other tribes. Perhaps the other tribe will not bother us. Perhaps the other tribe will send men to steal our corn before winter. I do not know. There may be danger. I must think very carefully and I will hold a tribal council with the other men, after I have done much thinking."

"Father, should we help the boy? Do we have enough corn to share with his village?"

"I don't know. Tehya, you must go get Akule right now. Go."

Tehya ran to Akule's house. He was outside dancing while holding part of an elk's antler above his head. "Akule, put that down. Please come now. Please come with me."

"I'll come. Let me put the antler in the house."

As the two children walked quickly through the village, Tehya explained that she had told her parents about the other tribe and about the hungry boy. Akule was silent. They entered Tehya's house.

"Father, here is Akule."

"Boy, you are a good friend. Was it your idea to go to the north hill?"

Akule was frightened but also brave. He spoke with a strong voice. "Yes, it was my idea. Tehya tried to tell me not to go, but I knew we would be careful and return safely. We did. I am sorry I made her disobey you."

"But, Akule, you might have frightened that strange boy and now his tribal people are worried about our tribe. This is a serious thing. I am not angry now. I must think. Akule, did you tell your parents about this or anybody else in the village?"

"No. I wanted to tell my friends, but I saw the look on Tehya's mother's face when we told her and knew it would not be a good idea to tell anyone."

"Tehya and Akule, you must promise me to not tell anyone about your visit to the other village until I have had my time to think and to have a council with the other men." Father put his large brown hand on the table and said, "Children, put your hands on my hand and look into my eyes. You must promise. Do you understand?"

"Yes, father, we will not tell anyone about the others or about their village or the boy."

Friends

As Tehya and Akule went outside, she thanked him for telling her father the truth. Tehya was so relieved that her father was not angrier. She knew he would know what to do about the other tribe to the north. Now she had a happy thought. She remembered what her mother had said about a baby sister and was anxious to tell Mansi. She told Akule she had to see Mansi and said goodbye.

Mansi was sitting in front of her house playing with her little sister who was about three-years-old. Suddenly, Tehya realized what a little sister meant. She had always taken Mansi's sister for granted as just a cute little child, but now she would have a sister of her own. As she approached, she waved to Mansi. "Mansi, I have a surprise. My mother has told me that she believes our new baby will be a girl."

Mansi's little sister jumped up and said joyfully, "A new baby…a new girl baby."

"Yes, a new girl baby," replied Tehya. "Mansi, what is it like to have a little sister?"

"It is fun, mostly. There is always someone to play with. And I am learning to be a mother when I take care of her. That's what mother said. You know that sometimes I can't play with you and Akule because of her. Sometimes she cries, but I just hug her and then walk away so she doesn't think I will do everything for her. She must grow up, too. Tehya, you will be a good sister and Hakan will be a good brother."

"Thanks, Mansi."

The Council of Men

The next morning, Tehya's father went from house to house to speak with each man in the village. He told them there would be a war council to discuss protecting the village if the winter was very harsh and more men came from other tribes to steal their food. This had not happened for many years because there had been plenty of rain and plenty of food. This year would be different. Every tribe would have a difficult time getting through the winter. This hardship could also bring serious danger.

The war council included nine men: three young men who were very strong and not married, three fathers with young children, and three grandfathers who were still strong. This way, many ideas would be heard and all the needs of the village would be considered. The reasons for the three groups of men were these: Young men of the village would be expected to go in the front of a war party and to take more risks. Their voices must be heard. The fathers with young children had much more to protect. Their voices must also be heard. The grandfathers were wise and had seen bad winters and wars before. They would teach the younger men of the learning of their ancestors and the best ways to make war if necessary. Some of the older men knew the strange words of the other tribes and could talk with them. Some tribes did not make war and would talk. Other tribes were angry tribes and would not talk. Of course, these were the tribes that worried Tehya's father.

It was time for the council. The nine men sat around a small fire. Tehya's father was the village war chief. He was a large man and very strong. He had learned of war from the older men. He led many great hunts but had only fought in one small war with 20 men who raided their village about the time Tehya was born. Father fought bravely to drive the strange men from the village. The other men saw and asked him to be the war chief. Now, he would truly be tested for wisdom, courage, and leadership.

The men began their meeting with a short chant that reminded them of their families—those who had lived in their land for many years before them. The chant reminded them of their love for the mountains that captured the snow to create the water spring…and the forest with the many animals that lived in it. Their land was a beautiful land and it gave them life. The Great Spirit gave them life by giving them their land. Next to their families, their land was the most precious thing.

When the chant was finished, a grandfather spoke. "This is a serious time. We must be very slow to make war. If our men are killed, our children will have no fathers. Men from the other tribe will come here and take our women."

A young man stood up. He spoke with an angry voice. "This is our land. No strange men can ever come here to take our women, our corn, our meat, or any other thing. We will be ready. If we must go to their villages first, we will be fierce. We will kill the young men of their villages, but not their old men. We will not take their women. This is not our way, but we will fight."

The council meeting continued into the evening. The other village men and women stood with their children near their houses and watched as the nine men of the council leaned forward, gestured, stood up, and moved around their fire. For Tehya, it was almost magical to see the nine dark shapes of men in the firelight. They looked more like ghosts or spirits to her. She wondered what they were saying.

Tehya's father spoke very little. After the stars had come out to cover the sky, he stood up and raised his arms and lowered them. Then he gave counsel to his fellow tribesmen: "My friends, young men, fathers, and grandfathers, you are brave and wise. Our people believe many things. We believe that life is given to each man and woman and child by God. No one should steal this gift from another. To kill others is not our way. We also believe that we must protect our children. It is only when others come to harm our children that we must fight. If we do not know for sure that the men of other tribes are angry with us and will come to harm us, we must leave them alone. We believe that their lands are their lands and their ways are their ways given to them by their ancestors. We also believe that we must be ready for hard times."

Tehya's father continued to speak. "We must end our meeting now. Tomorrow, we will begin to make new spears and to sharpen our old spears. We will practice the fighting so we are ready to protect our women and our children if this is necessary. We will also send three men to the north, three to the east, three to the south, and three men to the west to learn of the other tribes—where they are and what their movements are and about their preparations for winter or war. We must not go into their villages. I believe it is possible that some tribes are not ready for winter. Some are already hungry. If the problems of the other tribes are many, then it may be time for a great council of tribes before winter is here and any war begins."

Up to this point, the members of the council were impressed with their war chief's wisdom and his plan. However, when he mentioned a council of tribes, two of the grandfathers stood and tried to speak at the same time. The first to speak said, "When I was young and not yet a father, there was such a meeting of tribes. We met to discuss the water springs...to find water for all tribes. There was much searching for new water. New springs were found and each tribe had water. The tribes without enough water took the new water springs as their own. There was no war."

The second grandfather to stand now spoke. "I have been on the war council for many years. Some of you forgot that the tribe to the north came to our corn fields before to steal our food. We asked for a council of tribes to stop the stealing. Four tribes sent men to the meeting. Some tribes refused to join us. There were many strange words spoken that I could not understand. Some men began to shout and to push each other. The meeting was very bad. There were only threats of killing if any tribe took corn from another tribe. The men in that council said they would never meet again, that the meeting was foolish and each tribe should stay in its own land."

Tehya's father stood again. He said, "We will care for our families in our own land while we also make preparations to protect them. Before we go to any other village to make war, we will try to talk with the other tribes. Perhaps, I will go to the other villages if we must ask them to meet with us. This will be my test. Please go back to your families. We will meet again tomorrow morning."

Father returned to the house where his family was eager to hear what the war council had spoken. "Father," said Hakan, "Will there be a war before winter?"

"My son, go to bed. It is foolish to speak of such things. We do not know yet what the winter will bring. The men of our village will make preparations to protect our families. All women and children should keep working to prepare food and blankets for the winter. This is the only wise thing. Go to bed."

The family all went to their beds. As mother turned toward the wall to make herself comfortable, she spoke softly to her husband. "The baby will come soon."

Two Sounds

As the first morning sun shown through the window above Tehya's sleeping place, she awoke and rolled over. As she began to be conscious of the new day, she heard two sounds. The first was a scraping sound—many scraping sounds together. As she listened, she knew the sound was of stones striking stones. The men were sharpening their spears. Then she heard a soft whimpering sound. It was the sound of a baby.

Tehya jumped from her pile of blankets and ran to the other side of the wall. "Mother, Father, was a baby born? Is our baby sister here?"

Father was not there but Mother was sitting up amidst her blankets holding a small bundle next to her breasts. "Tehya, she came quickly in the night. She cried out and I was afraid she would wake you and Hakan. Father and I brought her here. It was so much easier than when you and Hakan were born. Come see."

Tehya tip toed over to her mother. Her mother turned the bundle around and said, "Tehya, this is your new sister, Yepa. Look outside. It is snowing. We will remember her as our snow maiden. She came softly in the night as the snow was beginning to fall. She is a peaceful baby. Take her. Hold her carefully."

The tiny baby was so sweet. Her eyes were closed tightly and the eyelids were pinched together and puffed up. She had such a small mouth and a nose just like a baby bunny. "Mother, I love her already."

"I know, Tehya. I have loved her for many months and now she is born."

"Mother, is father happy to have two daughters and only one son? Did he want Yepa to be a boy?"

"Yes, he is happy with two daughters. He says that one son is enough. He has one strong son who will walk by his side and he is happy with this. He told me that now there are three flowers in his house—three women to make it beautiful and this is good. He is very happy. Tehya, he knows you are strong. He and I know you will be a very special woman to help our people more and more as you grow older and wiser."

"Thank you, Mother."

The baby began to fuss and turn inward to nuzzle Tehya's night clothes. "Here, mother, she wants you."

Mother took the baby. Tehya smiled and hurried back to her bed. She changed her clothes and ran outside to tell her friends about her new sister. It was early in the morning. Perhaps they were still sleeping. She ran toward Mansi's house. As she did, she saw the men at work on their spears. Even amidst the happiness of Yepa's arrival, this sight made her sad. She knew these spears were not for hunting.

Reports from the Scouting Parties

As Father had told the war council, four groups of men were sent to the other lands to the north, west, south, and east. They were to observe each tribe from some distance and not enter their village.

The people of Tehya's village waited patiently to learn what these groups had discovered. The first group to return was from the north. Father asked them to wait until the other three groups came back. To Tehya and her friends, it seemed like a very long time before the other groups returned. The next to return was from the west and then the two groups from the south and east arrived. By the looks on the men's faces, it was easy to know that they were very tired. They had traveled far. When each group returned, father greeted them and told them there would be another war council meeting to hear their reports, after they had rested for a day.

The report meeting was held in the early morning and not around an evening fire as before. Father told the village he wanted everybody to think and to speak clearly just like the cool morning air under the blue fall sky. The war council sat in a circle ready to hear reports from each of the four groups. These are their reports...

North. "War council, we are the group that traveled to the north. As most of us know, there is a tribe very near us just over the first hill. This tribe is small. They were quiet. They were not sharpening spears. From a distance, they seemed to be sick because they walked very slowly. The children were smaller than our children. We think this tribe does not have much food for the winter. Beyond this first tribe, we found one other village. It, too, is small. We think the people there live in one large house with many rooms. We could see where their corn fields had been. These people were also busy. There was some singing. This is all we know."

West. "Good morning, mighty war chiefs; we are the group from the west. We went to the top of the western mountain to look for fire smoke. There was smoke from only one direction. When we traveled there, we found a large village. The houses are in many rows and these are big and beautiful houses. There were many men practicing for war. On one side of the village, behind the houses, there is a very large building like a house but not a house, with many hooks all around the outside walls. The people hung new spears on these hooks. The sound of many stones scraping was coming from inside. We know the spears are new because the women were sitting in groups rubbing the spear shafts to make them smooth. The village was making so many spears. This tribe is a tribe of warriors. The men practicing are fierce. And, we noticed that they held their spears in one hand. On the other hand, each warrior had a circle of wood tied on with a leather strap. This is to protect from the spears enemies throw at them. We must make these circles of wood to protect our warriors. There was not much singing, but there were war chants in the morning and dancing before the sun went down behind the trees. These people are strong. There was much meat drying on poles outside each house."

South. "We are the group from the south. We found only one tribe. This tribe is not like the tribes to the north. They are not hungry. They did not practice fighting. The most interesting thing to us is the many tree poles they have placed around their land. On these poles there are markings—their tribal marks—and some men walk along these poles each day and look from the east to the west and from north to south. All the children wore the same color of white cloth around their waists. Each morning, the children would walk together to one big house where two or three women would teach them, together, not as our mothers teach our children in our own houses. These people were not practicing for war, but their village is very well protected from outsiders by the watchers and the many poles. It would be hard to steal seed corn from this village."

East. Finally, the group that had traveled to the east gave their report. "We have a very curious report for the war chiefs. There are two villages to the east. They are the same in some ways, but different. The men of these tribes do not have spears. They have strange long knives and they practice a war dance quickly around each other in circles as they poke these long knives at each other. The women cover their heads. We believe the families spend much time together. These are large families. They have a Spirit Man, but he stands on a tall wooden tower to speak many prayers. They pray to God often. There was not so much meat on poles in these villages. There were small antelope gathered inside a field surrounded by short wooden poles. The children would bring these animals dried grass to eat. We saw one family kill a small antelope and share it with other families. We looked closely at their corn fields, but we did not find corn. There were small seeds that we have never seen before. The curious thing about the two villages is that each morning some men from one village climb to a small hill nearby and watch the other village. Men from the other village do the same. The villages are similar but no one traveled between the two villages. There was just watching."

Tehya's father, the war chief, arose. "Thank you all brave men who have journeyed to these faraway places. There are so many interesting tribes. I have this question. Were their faces strange and was the color of their skin the same as our color?"

Several men spoke almost at once with common answers, "We were never close enough to know the look of their faces or the color of their skins. From a distance, their villages appear to be similar to our own. There are houses, women with children, men watching or practicing for war. We could not tell how much food each tribe has stored. We think that each tribe has their own way that is the best way for them."

One man from the north group stepped forward and said, "I can agree that this is true except for the village most near to us on the other side of the north hill. Their way is not working. They will be hungry this winter. They need a better way for finding meat and growing corn. Their children are very thin and sad, I think."

The war chief spoke. "Thank you. The war council will now discuss together what we have learned and make our decision."

The discussions that followed lasted for many hours. The children went back to their play. The men and women of the village returned to their work. The men of the council did not eat. As the war council discussions came to their conclusion, three things were most interesting. There was much fear of the tribe to the west. This tribe's many warriors and weapons made the council feel justified in preparing for war.

The two tribes to the east were so different from other tribes these men had ever seen that they did not know what conclusion to reach. Even the grandfathers had not heard of such strange prayers and keeping small antelope inside a field surrounded by short poles or women who covered their heads.

Finally, there was some worry for the tribe to the north, mixed with frustration that the men of that village did not hunt for more meat to feed their children. Perhaps the fathers and mothers of that village were not strong enough to hunt. If there was some sickness in the village, this would be an explanation. The men knew that once a tribe became weak, their situation would quickly become worse until it was too late. One of the grandfathers knew of a tribe far away, many years ago, that had many people die from a strange sickness.

Tehya's father spoke again. "My friends, there are two plans we can make and we must choose one of these. One plan is to stay in our own land and prepare for war and to protect our families. But, there are now many more tribes nearby than ever before. Perhaps we cannot ignore these other tribes. Sooner or later, they will come to us for food or to make war. The other plan is to create a great council of tribes, once again, to know the many needs of these tribes and to teach each other new ways. All the tribes can gather more food and hunt elk so there will be plenty for all and no need to steal or to be afraid.

The council members mumbled. One of them spoke. "This can be tried, our chief, but when you speak of plenty for all, you do not understand how many bad men wish to kill us and steal from us. They do not care about our tribe, only their tribes. You do not realize how many dangers there are. We can get the sickness from the village to the north. The strange ways of the villages to the east will confuse our children. We should leave all tribes alone, in their own lands."

Their war chief listened. He leaned his head to the left and then to the right before he gave his decision. "We must try to have peace with the other tribes. We must try this once for our children so they will not see the blood of war. I will take two men with me, a young warrior and a grandfather. We will take our dried berries and our finest nuts as gifts and go to the other villages. We will cover our backs with a white cloth so they know we are not trying to hide from them. I will take a beautiful knife made from the elk's antler for each chief and a shiny stone like the one my wife wears for the wife of each chief. Our grandfather who will travel with me can speak words that many other tribes understand—words to say that we invite each chief to come to our village to eat, to see our dancing, and to talk. If they come, it will be good to see each other eye to eye. If they do not come, then we will leave them alone and pray that no war comes. This is my decision."

Father's Journeys

Tehya and Hakan and their mother were very worried to learn that Father was preparing to travel to all of the surrounding tribes. What if he frightened them and they hurt him or killed him or took him as their prisoner? There was no peace on earth that was worth losing their father, they thought.

Father chose two very brave men to join him—one older and one younger. The older man was called Demothi. The young man was Helaku. They made many preparations. They would take the same paths the four scouting groups had taken and make four separate trips so they could return to the village for fresh supplies after traveling north, then west, south, and east.

The time came for Father and the other men to leave. There were tears shed in the privacy of their homes and many hugs. Mother was so brave. She told her children that their father had been chosen to make peace with the other tribes. The Great Spirit had chosen him, so he would go with the blessings of heaven to help him and protect him. Mother said she was sure he would return safely. The children believed in the faith of their mother.

On the morning of the first journey to the other tribes, all the people of Tehya's tribe met in the center of the village where the fire meetings were held. The people lined up in front of several houses in a straight line so that Father and his two companions could walk by each of them to hear their individual wishes and know of their prayers for a safe journey.

The three men traveled far and learned much. These are the stories of their visits to the other tribes. Three tribes (west, south, and east) were most unique in their own ways and therefore had the most significant influence on the events that were to follow Father's visits to their villages. The fourth tribe was the tribe to the north that was suffering from hunger and other problems. This tribe was at great risk with the winter approaching. This is the report from the north.

North

As Father and his friends approached the village, they could see that word was spreading among the people that strangers were coming. Soon four men appeared from inside one of the houses nearest the entrance to the village. These men walked confidently toward the three strangers they had been warned were coming. By some instinct, these four men and Father with his companions stopped about one small tree length apart. Demothi spoke a few words to the four men from the village. They smiled and nodded their heads. Father stepped carefully forward with a beautiful elk horn knife wrapped in a piece of soft leather. He said, "For your chief." The oldest of the four men walked toward Father and reached out his hand. He took the knife and nodded his appreciation. Demothi told of the great tribal council meeting to be held on the long night that would begin the winter.

The chief turned back around to face his village. He whistled and waved toward his people who were standing in the distance watching. As soon as he whistled, several small children came running—two boys and three girls. The children were smiling, but they did not look well. They were thin and were breathing heavily after running from the village. The old chief went to one of the boys, knelt down, pulled up the boy's leather tunic and pointed to his ribs and then rubbed his sunken belly. The chief looked up at the three visitors and gently shook his head.

Father, Demothi, and Helaku looked at each other and gently shook their heads. Helaku stepped back a few feet to where his carry sack was laying. He reached in and recovered a large portion of dried meat that was wrapped in a coarse cloth. He walked back to the chief and handed him the meat. Demothi then explained that when the great tribal council met, the many chiefs would talk about the hungry children so they would not suffer and die in the coming winter. The old chief continued staring up at his three guests. His eyes were very wet. He said in his own language, "I will come on the long night. The Great Spirit has sent you. Thank you for coming to our village."

Father and his companions returned to their village. Everyone was excited to see them and to know if the tribes to the north would come to the tribal council meeting. Father explained that there are two tribes and they eventually visited both villages. However, it is the tribe just over the north hill that is in serious danger of starvation and needs help or some of their children will die. As Tehya heard this report, she worked her way through the crowd to her father's side. She waited patiently while he finished talking and walked with him to their house. As they walked, she said, "Father, you have been where Akule and I have been. Perhaps the boy you saw was our friend who is hungry. Father, please help him."

"Tehya, Helaku gave them some meat. We will find a way to help."

West

After one day's rest at home and with fresh supplies, Father, Demothi, and Helaku left for the village to the west. This journey required that they climb one mountain and then descend into a vast valley. They could see many smoke fires in the distance where they knew the village to be. As they came closer and closer, they could hear war chants. They knew they were about to encounter a mighty nation that could intimidate other tribes. The earlier scouting party had prepared them for the warlike nature of this tribe and also observed that the village was very orderly. Perhaps they would be greeted only with formality and not with violence.

In fact, Father and his companions were soon alarmed to see a large party of warriors appear on the horizon. They were marching rapidly up and over the crest of a small hill just ahead of them. The men were wearing bright colors across they bodies. All the warriors' tunics were identical with two colored stripes that cut diagonally across each tunic from the left shoulder to the right side of their bodies. One of the men was carrying a tall pole to which was attached a large cloth with the same stripes. Father was both impressed and frightened. Demothi, Helaku, and he stood very still and waited.

A very large man walked toward them with his right hand held to the square. He smiled and appeared friendly. Demothi greeted him with a few short words known to many tribes. The large man turned completely around, with his hand still in the air. He simultaneously motioned to his guests that they should follow him and that his warriors should turn around and march back to the village.

The village was straight ahead. What Father and his companions saw next was utterly amazing to them. The village was huge. There were neat clusters of big, beautiful houses. In the center of the main pathway through the village there were large wooden racks. As they drew closer, Father noticed that these racks were the resting place for many spears of many different sizes and shapes. It appeared that these were on display to impress visitors to the village. There were spears too large for one man to carry. Such spears had to be carried by two or three warriors. These could only be needed to kill a huge bear or perhaps to break through the door of a house and frighten those who lived in it. Around the edges of the village, there were many, many racks with dried meat. There were women in large groups cutting and sewing leather. Huge piles of clothing lay on tables nearby. The women wore their own bright colors and had many shiny stones hanging around their necks. Father had never seen such organization or so much food or so much preparation for war.

The large man guided them to the end of the village. There was a wonderful feast prepared. Now father knew that his arrival with Demothi and Helaku had been anticipated. This tribe had been watching them cross the valley and was ready for their visit.

The large man spoke. He startled them by speaking in their language. These were his words, "We are happy that you have come to our village. We have prepared food for you. There has been word sent to us that you are speaking with other tribes about a great tribal council meeting. We will have such a meeting in our village and you will come."

Father spoke. "Great chief, we thank you for your food. Your village is beautiful. Your people are well organized. We are happy that you want to join the council meeting. It has been our plan to hold such a meeting in our village to the east on the long night when winter begins."

"No, that will not be necessary," said the large man. "We have many tables, much food, and will make the council meeting easy for you. You must come here. You will bring your family. My wife will make a house for your family and food and blankets. They will be our guests."

Father turned to his companions. The three of them were all surprised by this reception and at first could not speak. Father turned back to the powerful chief and indicated that he must talk with his friends. He then spoke in a moderate voice to Demothi and Helaku: "I think we must come to this village. These people are powerful and we must not make them angry. If they do not come to the meeting, it will be dangerous. If we go to their village, perhaps they will listen to our plan and bring much wood and leather and food to help the other villages in the winter months."

Father agreed with the chief that his village in the west would be the place for the tribal council. A meal and dancing followed. Father, Demothi, and Helaku rested one night and left the next morning to return to their own land. They did not talk much as they traveled. Their feeling was that the large man had too much power and that he really did not want to hear their ideas. Father realized he had not given the large man a gift. He should have done this, but he knew his elk horn knife would have been too small a gift for such a great chief.

South

Father, Demothi, and Helaku returned to their village, but did not stay long—just one night. The three men soon began their journey to the south village, which was not so far away. As they came upon the village, there were people working and some children playing. This time, the three men knew they had surprised the tribe they were about to visit. Their appearance as strangers caused these villagers to grab their tools and children and run. As they witnessed this fearful reaction, Father, Demothi, and Helaku immediately sat down in the dirt, crossed their legs, and bowed their heads. This was a sign of "no danger;" that they had come in peace. They sat for a long time. Finally, a woman came walking toward them from the village. She was smiling and holding her arms out in front of her. As she approached, she sat down near her guests. She said, "Welcome to our village. We believe you come in peace." Demothi told her of their purpose. Father presented her with a shiny stone on its leather string. She took it and bowed her head toward them.

Father told Demothi to ask her why there were so many poles in straight lines around their fields and why men walked back and forth along these poles. She replied, "This is our land that we have marked. We do not make war as long as no one takes land that we have marked with the poles." She then pointed to the far corner of one field. "Those far away poles point to new lands that do not belong to any other tribes. Each year, we take new land and put poles there to mark it. As our mothers have more children, we need more land. We count the children and we know how much land we will need. Then we mark it."

Demothi asked her about their chief. Her answer: "My husband is the chief. He is very busy making plans for our new land and has sent me."

"Will he come to the great tribal council meeting?"

"I believe he will come. He will bring two more chiefs. One chief is for our land to the west and the other chief is for our land to the east. I am the one who counts the children when they are born and knows how much food and leather there is in our storehouse. My husband will ask me to come to the council meeting. We will tell the other tribes which lands belong to our tribe. We can help other tribes make a plan for their lands."

Father nodded his approval. Then he explained that the council meeting would be held at the large village to the west over the mountain.

The chief's wife spoke. "It is a long journey, but we are happy that you and the other chiefs will not come here. There would be too many people who would trample our fields and we do not have guesthouses for strangers. We will go to the west as you say."

This completed the third major visit to the other tribes. The now weary threesome once again returned to their village. There was one thing that brought much contentment to them, after all of their preparation and so much travel. So far, every tribe had greeted them with friendliness and was willing to participate in the great tribal council.

East

Now, the journey to the east began. Father and Demothi and Helaku were most curious about the people to the east. As far as Father knew, none of his people had met with these tribes before, not even the oldest grandfathers. After two days travel, they hoped they would soon arrive at the village. They thought they saw fire smoke. Then, before they could see the village, they heard a distant voice that was chanting that sounded like a prayer to the Great Spirit. The voice was high-pitched and very much unlike the deep and monotone voice of their tribe's spirit man. The prayer was repeated and then all was very quiet. They did not hear the voice again until after they reached the village. The words of the chant were words they had never heard in any other village. Even Demothi did not recognize the language.

The most noticeable thing about this east village was the tall tower just inside the village entrance. As they got closer to the village, they could see a man in the tower. They thought he was a watcher. Then, the prayer chanting began again. The sound came from the tower. They now realized the tower was there to make the man's voice easy to hear from all around the village and even far away in the forest where they had first heard it.

A man came walking from the village. He was not dressed like the other chiefs. He did not wear any leather but wore only a long white gown, like women sometimes wear. He beckoned them to approach. The man had a full dark beard and his skin was the color of the antelope's back just as Father had heard the travelers tell in their stories of faraway lands. Father noticed the color because it was not like the color of his own skin, which was the color of the summer earth after the rain.

Demothi tried to speak to the man, but there was no understanding. The man spoke his strange words. Demothi could only shake his head gently from left to right. The man turned and motioned that the four of them should walk together to the village.

As they entered the village, the men noticed that the houses were made of mud bricks and very little wood. Men of the village came forward and nodded at them as they walked by. It was strange that the women stood in the background. The heads of the women were covered with cloths that hung down over their shoulders. As any man would turn toward any woman, she would take the cloth that hung from her head and cover her face, except for her eyes. The village was very quiet.

In the center of the village was a very large house with a round roof. As they approached, an older man with a dark beard came out. All the men had beards, it seemed. The older man, who was apparently the chief, motioned that his three guests should sit down just outside the large house on two stone benches. Again, Demothi attempted to communicate without any success. All the men could do was smile at each other and courteously nod their heads up and down. Father sat his carry sack down on the ground and opened it. He carefully withdrew an elk horn knife and a shiny stone with its leather string. He held these out to the chief. The chief smiled and shook his head. He then motioned to a man and a woman to come and stand beside him. As the two of them walked over to their chief and his three guests, the man opened his white dress to reveal a large curved knife; then he quickly covered it up. The chief stood up and gestured to the woman's neck and shook his head. Father noticed that the woman wore no stones or colors of any kind.

The chief reached out his hand to Father's hand. Father was surprised. Normally, he only took the hand of his wife or his daughter, not the hand of a man, but he knew he must take this chief's hand. The chief led him toward a small house. Demothi and Helaku followed. Just to the right of the entrance to the house was another stone bench with bowls of food placed on it. As Father looked inside the house, he saw many neatly folded blankets.

The chief smiled and walked away. His people followed him leaving Father, Demothi, and Helaku alone. Father and his companions knew the food was for them. It was unusual food, but tasty. The men were very hungry. As soon as they ate, they went inside the house to sleep. As the sun went down, they heard that voice again, coming from the tower. The chanting prayers were repeated and then stopped. All was quiet.

Father was awakened the next morning by another chanting prayer. He now knew that these people spent much time thinking of the Great Spirit. Perhaps they feared wild animals or a warring tribe nearby or perhaps they had sick children or not enough food for the winter. He did not know why they prayed so much. It was the way of his people to pray as a village when there was a serious need or a celebration. Other prayers were said quietly inside their houses among their own family members. These were mostly to thank God for plenty of food and good health and for new babies.

There was a knocking sound on the wall of the house. Father walked outside and there was the village chief. He knew he must find a different way to speak to this new friend. He took the chief's hand and led him back to the two benches outside the big house with the round roof. They sat down. Father picked up a stick and drew in the dirt. He drew two pictures. The first was the crude sketch of a village with small houses and one big house with a round roof in the center of the village. To the right, and toward the west, Father drew a second village with an arrow sign pointing from east to west between the two villages to suggest a journey between them. These objects were all part of Father's first drawing. Next, he drew a small sun shape and a large half-moon shape. He hoped this would communicate the idea of a short day and a long night to suggest the timing of a journey between the east and west villages.

The chief stood up. He appeared to be very happy. He thumped his chest and then pointed to the west. He marched a few steps forward and then back again, swinging his arms vigorously. He pretended to hold a spear and thrust it. Father now knew the chief and his people must already be aware of the large village to the west with its many warriors. He was finally communicating with the chief.

The old chief sat down on the other bench. Then, he lay down on his side and pretended to be asleep. As he slept, he counted with his fingers over and over again. Father knew he understood "long night." When the chief sat up they both nodded. The chief took his hand briefly. They walked back to the house to awaken Demothi and Helaku.

After morning food, the chief led them back to the village entrance, past the tall prayer tower, and nodded a polite farewell.

Father knew there was another similar village nearby. He hoped the old chief had understood his invitation and would tell the other village of their visit and bring the neighboring chief to the tribal council as well. It was very difficult to communicate with these people in the east. Their ways were so different, but Father knew their ways were especially important to them.

Mission Accomplished

Father, Demothi, and Helaku headed home for the last time. This had been a very big challenge for them—to communicate with so many people in so many places.

The children saw them coming. Tehya led the way as a small throng of children eventually surrounded the three weary travelers. "Father, will they come? Will the chiefs from the other tribes come to the great tribal council meeting?"

"Tehya, I think they will come. Perhaps not all will come, but enough will come that we can have an agreement about the winter and the needs of many of the people in this big land." Father paused. "I sometimes think we are all one tribe and God is the big chief of this tribe. Tehya, how are your mother and baby sister?"

"Father, they are well. The baby is fat. Mother feeds her too much, I think."

Preparation

When the new day arrived, father walked around and around the inside and the outside of his family's house. He looked at the roof. He examined the firewood stacked behind the house. Inside, he counted the blankets and looked inside each pot and sack that held food. He also checked his spears and replaced them carefully on hooks near the ceiling in the room where he and mother slept. He did not want the children to play with these spears. Tehya knew that her father was preparing for winter and had many ways to protect their family.

That night at dinner, Father explained that the great tribal council meeting would be soon, on the longest night when the winter begins. He also told the family that the meeting would not be in their village but in the large village to the west. They would journey with him and be guests of the chief's wife in that village. Mother was worried.

"Father, is it wise to take our baby so far away? What if these people take us as their prisoners and we cannot return to our village?"

Father reminded her that she had once told him that the work he was doing was because the Great Spirit wanted him to do it and that God would protect him. "Mother, God will protect all of us on this journey."

Tehya and Hakan were very excited. "Father," said Tehya, "Will the other villages help the hungry village and the boy who is so thin? Will they know that they do not need to steal or to make a war?"

"My daughter, we can only pray to the Great Spirit that all the chiefs and their people will understand these things. We have much to do to get ready for our journey. Help your mother."

Waiting and Walking

It seemed to Tehya that it would be too many days before the journey to the west. She was ready to go and did not want to wait. She counted the days and kept herself busy helping her mother sew new clothes for the family. She and her friends would try to imagine what the other tribes must be like. Father had given her permission to talk about the tribe to the north, but he had forbidden her to take other children there. Perhaps, after the great tribal council meeting, it would be safer to make friends with the people of this humble village. Father also wanted to be sure there was not a sickness that the children would bring back to their own village.

It was the day before the long journey to the west would begin. There was much excitement in the village. Many families came to Tehya's house to give their blessings to her family. Some brought gifts to give to the representatives of the other tribes they would meet. Some offered to give food to the north tribe if the chiefs of the great tribal council approved. Tehya was so impressed by the genuine curiosity and the generosity of her people.

Finally, the morning Tehya had been waiting for arrived. The family ate, put on their warmest clothing, filled their carry sacks, and set out for the village to the west. Several other members of the village accompanied them to carry the gifts and the extra supplies Tehya's family required because they were a family with younger children who could not carry everything themselves. These other friends included Demothi who would be very important as a translator of languages.

The journey began under a clear sky and walking toward the west mountain was easy. On the second day of the journey, the mountain grew closer and the skies grew darker. Tehya knew there would be snow. She could feel on her skin the difference between coming rain and snow in the air. There was already some snow on the mountain. Tehya was excited to have more snow. As the family and their supporters climbed the mountain, a heavy snow began to fall. Soon they were walking in snow midway up the calves of their legs. Father decided to make a trail that would cut across the base of the mountain to the north so they could cross on a low ridge and not have to climb too steeply. This was a good idea. Tehya and Hakan had begun to get very tired walking up the mountain in the deepening snow.

With the change in the weather, Father decided to camp in a narrow canyon near the mountain ridge. They would be protected from the weather and not have to cross the ridge in the dim twilight. One of the other villagers found a large overhanging rock under which they could camp and build more shelter. They placed broken tree branches and some small trees against the outcropping of the rock and then placed pine bows over the wood frame to keep out the snow. They built a fire. With plenty of blankets, it was a cozy evening with snow falling and the fire flickering. Tehya felt that she was living in a dream. She imagined that angels were guiding them toward heaven on the other side of the mountain and that her father would become the great chief of all tribes with her mother at his side. She would be a princess. As she looked out through cracks in their shelter to see the stars mixed with sparks from the fire, Tehya's sense of something magical increased. Then, her eyelids became heavy and she realized it was not a dream, but an imagining. She fell asleep.

Tehya was awakened by the baby crying. Mother was standing inside the shelter rocking the baby. It was very cold. Father was outside building a new fire. Tehya and Hakan got dressed and went outside. The sky was blue and they were in a winter land that looked like Tehya's heavenly dream. The world was white with only a few tree tops peeking up from the snowy blanket that covered everything else. Father told the children to wrap their legs in their special leather stockings to keep out the snow. He and the other men would go ahead to mark a path in the snow so the family could follow with less effort. The world was beautiful, but this part of the journey was more difficult.

Because it was late fall and not the middle of winter, the midday sun was warm and as the group crossed over the mountain ridge, the snow began to melt quickly. There was less snow on the other side of the mountain and the ground was rockier, so the walking became easier. Off in the distance they could see fire smoke. The village that was the source of the smoke was across the wide valley, but it seemed close to Tehya because she now had a clear destination in mind and she knew they would be traveling across level ground.

No Longer a Faraway Place

The family and friends arrived at the west village. Tehya and Hakan were amazed by its size and by the number of people moving about. To Tehya, it seemed that there were 10 of her villages gathered here in one place. Children came out to greet them. They were playful just like Tehya and Hakan's friends back home. All the children were immediately swept up in some game of running and chasing each other—some universal game children instinctively play. Father wondered at their ability to relate to each other so quickly and without understanding each others' languages.

Father saw the large man who was chief motioning to other children to go and greet his guests from their neighboring village—the one he called "the village where many paths cross." This was true. The location of Tehya's village was near a meadow where many paths crossed from one village to another. This is why her people knew of so many other tribes and hoped to unite them as the peoples of one great land.

Father met the chief. They placed their hands on each others' elbows in a special greeting that showed both friendship and firmness. This was a man's greeting. Today, it was a chief's greeting. Father looked for Demothi and saw him nearby. He motioned that he needed Demothi's language translating help. Demothi came and greeted the west village chief. Father directed him to inquire about the other tribes. The chief motioned to one large house nearby.

Meanwhile, Mother had been resting on a wooden bench with the baby. Father excused himself and briefly went to her. Just as he did, he saw the village chief's wife walking rapidly toward them. Almost in an instant she was standing at Mother's side and then escorting her two guests—mother and baby—toward the other end of the village where the chief's especially large house was situated. Father rejoined the chief and Demothi as they walked to the nearby house.

As they stepped inside the house, Father noticed the old chief from the north village. He saw the woman who was the wife of the chief to the south. Sitting next to her was a man of middle age. He immediately stood up and approached Father with the woman at his side. Demothi greeted the couple in their language. The chief of the south expressed his thanks for being included in the great tribal council meeting. He also turned and thanked his wife for having had the first conversation with Father when he had come to their village earlier. Father was very pleased. His host, chief of the west village, then motioned for several other men to stand. These men were chiefs of other smaller villages who had heard of the important meeting from neighboring villages and had decided to participate. They stood and introduced themselves. Father learned that most of them had brought family members and friends as he had done.

Father was almost overwhelmed. He did not know there were so many villages and he did not expect so many tribal leaders to participate in the tribal council. This would be a great meeting, he was sure. At the same time, he realized that an important chief was missing—the chief of the east village. He had Demothi ask their host about the chief of the east. The reply was, "This chief came yesterday with his wife, some other men and more women, and his children. There are many children. They asked to have a separate house to have a special place to pray. Now is their prayer time. They told me they will join us soon. At first, we could not speak with them. Their language is very strange to us. But, there is one man from the north village who knows their words." Father was relieved.

At Father's request, Demothi inquired further, "Is this chief of the east village pleased to be here even though there are so many other chiefs with different ways from his own?"

"Yes, he is happy, but he did tell us that his people would remain separate from the main village and that his children would play by themselves. They are a curious people, but they are also a generous people. We notice that they are very anxious to meet the old people of our village. They offer to help them walk and to give them food. They told me they have already taken food to the people of the north village who are very thin and tired and poor."

Father was so pleased. That night, as they returned to their guest quarters, he was filled with anticipation. Tehya, Hakan, Mother, and even their baby sister could feel their father's excitement. He spoke of a vast land where many chiefs would decide together and make peace for all the people. He spoke of the powerful warriors of the west village and how much he admired their spears. At the same time, he knew that so many spears were a contradiction to his plan for peace. When men had so many good spears, they were sometimes quick to make war. His biggest challenge would be to get many men to love peace more than their spears.

Mother told Father to stop talking and let the children sleep. Hakan complained, "Mother, let Father talk, please. This is a time of history. We can't sleep."

Father said, "Your mother is right, we must sleep."

Tehya asked, "Father, is the big meeting of the chiefs tomorrow morning?"

"No, daughter, there is first a morning feast so that we will all have full bellies and warm hands. There will be time for people of the many tribes to talk and to make friendships. At midday, there will be a prayer circle for all tribes. Afterwards, we will dance and play until dinner. Children will go to their beds early. Then, the big meeting will begin. Tehya and Hakan, you must go to sleep now."

"I have one more question, father," continued Tehya. "Mother has said that I have a special way and will someday help our tribe. Akule and I met the boy from the north village before your journey to the tribes. We want to know these other people and their ways and help them. Please, may Hakan and I stay in the shadows and listen to the chiefs talk—just for a short time, until the moon hides behind the trees?"

"Tehya, I will think on this. Go to sleep now."

The BIG Day

Many men and women arose before the sun came up. They had lit many fires to warm people of the village and their important guests. Tehya could smell meat roasting and corn cakes baking. She was excited.

As the children of the village awoke, the excitement grew. Children were running everywhere. Some of the girls were dancing. Boys were wrestling. Tehya sat on a log outside their guest house and watched these many interesting people. She had not noticed before, but as she sat quietly watching, she did realize that the looks of the many tribal people were in some ways the same but different. The people of each tribe smiled and walked in the same ways and worried about their busy children, but some had round faces and some longer faces. Some had skin the color of the brown earth, others had skin the color of the antelope's back. Some wore bright colors. The people of the east wore plain clothing. They were all so interesting. She thought that these people were like the many flowers that grow in the spring—some tall, some short, some red, some yellow, some with short petals, others with large drooping petals.

Tehya noticed her father moving among all the people. He was tall and handsome and so strong. Tehya felt so much love and admiration for him. He was nodding to each person he met and smiling. He would stop to talk with those of each tribe to make friends and show them where to find food and water and anything else they needed. Tehya thought that her father was like the honey bee in the spring going from flower to flower. Maybe he would become the great chief of all tribes.

As Father came towards Tehya, their eyes met and he knew he must spend a few minutes with this unusual and very special young woman. Father sat down next to her. "Tehya,

I am proud of you. You are wise beyond your years. This is a very proud thing for your father."

"Father, you are a friend to all the people. Will you become the great chief of all tribes?"

"No, Tehya, this is not my wish. I love our village and wish to stay there with you, your mother, Hakan, and baby sister. It is my wish that the many chiefs will respect each other and meet each year at this same time to decide together how we will live in this beautiful land God has given us all."

"Thank you, Father. I love you, Father" He put his arm around her and she rested her head on his chest.

The Prayer Circle

As the breakfast finished and the sun rose high in the sky, the large man who was chief of the west village and Father walked together to the center of the village and climbed up onto a platform that had been built of wood to help the people see and hear their chiefs when they spoke. The chief of the west raised his hands in the air and held them there. Mothers saw and told their children to stop running and to be quiet. The people slowly gathered at the center of the village. Their chief spoke and said, "There will now be a prayer for all people to ask God to bless our lands—all of our lands as one great land. We know that each tribe has its own way to pray, but as guests of my village, I ask you to listen to our spirit man as he prays in our way to bless all of you and your families."

The spirit man of the west village was dressed in many colors with a beautiful wreath of eagle feathers around his head. He held a large pole with the head of an eagle carved at the top. He raised his hands with one hand holding the pole. He looked toward the sun and spoke with a loud voice. This is his prayer...

"Great Spirit, listen to our prayer. We are many people with different ways. We must talk of many things. The winter will be hard. Some tribes have food, some do not have enough. We must find new ways for many tribes in this land or there will be stealing and we will have war. We pray for these things...words to speak to each other...much snow to fall in the mountains this winter so that there will be enough water for our corn fields in the spring and much grass for the antelope. Great Spirit, we pray for our children that they will follow the ways of their parents and be strong and learn many things of this world and of the spirit world so that they may live in peace. Father of All Spirits, we need words to speak, snow in our mountains, and healthy children. This is our prayer."

Hakan was sitting next to his sister and whispered, "He spoke of three things: *words, snow,* and *children.* Are these the most important things for all tribes or do the tribes have different things they need?"

"Hakan, it does not matter if these tribes are from the north, west, south, or east, they all have needs that are the same. Without *words* to speak at this meeting, there will be confusion and maybe war. Without *snow*, there will be no food and we will all die of hunger. And, without *healthy children*, there will be no future."

As the prayer ended, the spirit man lowered his hands to shoulder height and made a circular motion with his arms to suggest that the people could once again mingle and let their children play. Then, there was music. There were drum sounds and sticks clicking together. At the far end of the village, people were gathering as some began to sing. Tehya and Hakan joined the procession.

As the large gathering occurred, a group of people of the west village moved to the center of the crowd; formed themselves into a circle and began to dance. After their dance, they stepped back and opened their arms to invite other tribes to dance or to sing. The chief of the north with his wife, children, and followers came to the center and all began to sing. Their singing was not the chanting sound Tehya knew best. They sang softly in a together way that was like the sound of the water spring moving over the rocks that was so peaceful for Tehya.

There was more dancing. Tehya noticed the dancing and the singing of each tribe was curious and different and yet beautiful and interesting. When these many peoples were eating, praying, and dancing together, there was peace and friendship.

A Child is Lost

All was well, it seemed. Then, suddenly, the wife of the chief of the east came running out of the forest on the edge of the village. She was sobbing deeply and could hardly speak. The singing and dancing immediately stopped. Other women came and comforted this frightened mother. Through her tears she said, "My youngest child is lost. She has gone into the forest. My husband is looking for her. Her brothers and sisters are searching the village to find her. She is not here."

There was a new kind of energy in the village. Tehya could feel many tribes become one in just a moment. The men raised their hands to speak and to form groups to search for the child. Many groups would search in many different directions. Mothers comforted their smallest children and kept them nearby so they would not become lost amidst the frenzy that also engulfed the village.

Mother stayed to care for Yepa and other small children. Tehya and Hakan went with their father to look for the child. As the sun began to set in the west, Tehya knew the lost child would become very cold and could not survive alone in the forest. She was worried and she said her own prayer to the Great Spirit as she walked and searched.

The searching continued until it was almost dark.

Then, there was a loud shouting voice coming from the village: "We have found her. We have found her." The searchers in the forest now shouted to each other, "They have found her. She is safe. Return to the village."

When Father, Hakan, and Tehya returned to the village, the people were gathered around the special platform in its center. On the platform steps were the mother and her child who had been found. The mother was crying and then smiling and then crying again. Her words of thanksgiving were foreign to people of the other tribes but they could see the message of gratitude in her eyes and on her face. She reached out and hugged the women who surrounded her one by one.

As Tehya watched intently, she noticed a small, thin boy standing near the grateful mother. As the crowd became quieter, the woman turned and knelt beside the boy and hugged him. Tehya knew the boy. He was from the north village. She poked Hakan and motioned toward the scene now unfolding near the center platform. "Look," she said, "That's our friend from the north village."

A loud whisper now traveled through the crowd. "That little boy found the child. He's the one who found her. She was not far away but had crawled into a small cave. The little boy could see her low and crouching in the cave. Others had walked by too quickly. He heard her soft cry and found her."

Tehya knew this was a miracle. Two things were making her smile as she had never smiled before. She was amazed at how quickly many people had become as one tribe to save one child. She was amazed at the importance of one child.

Tehya turned to share her thoughts with Hakan, but he was gone. She looked left and right and could not find him. The crowd began to move away from the center platform. People were speaking softly and walking slowly. Mothers were holding their babies especially close. Fathers were telling their children to stay out of the forest and that it would soon be time for bed.

A Precious Gift

As Tehya walked back to their guest house, she noticed Hakan coming toward her holding something in his hand. He looked at her and smiled.

"What's in your hand, Hakan?"

"It is my bear claw."

"Why do you want a bear claw now, silly boy?"

"Tehya, I must give it to the boy from the north village. He has shown courage. He is a good boy. He cares for other children. He does not smile very much and this bear claw will make him smile. Come with me to find him."

The two children searched for their friend and found him with his family near the food tables. They were sitting together quietly eating the corn cakes that remained. As they approached, the boy stood up and the chief of the north village stood up. The three children nodded to each other. The boy spoke with simple words Tehya and Hakan could understand, "This is my grandfather."

Hakan spoke just a few words. "You have courage. You are our friend. This is for you." Hakan handed his friend the polished bear claw on its leather strap. The young boy smiled a smile so wide that it looked as if his face would split in two. His grandfather smiled.

At the other end of the village, a fire was beginning to grow and to fill the night sky with golden light. Soon it would be time for the meeting of chiefs. This would be a time of history.

The BIG Meeting

The fire burned down. Its red embers could be seen from a distance. Those who tended the fire put just enough wood on to keep a circle around it well lit and warm without sending too many sparks into the sky. The people of the village and their guests watched as the dark silhouettes of their chiefs appeared around the fire. One by one the chiefs filed into the circle and took their seats. There was no speaking. Tehya knew from watching the men of her village that it was the way of men to wait—to not be the first to speak and to reveal their thoughts too soon. However, once they began talking, there would be a rapid exchange of ideas and usually arguing.

Father had told Tehya and Hakan that they could sit at the edge of the forest near the fire circle. They must stay in the shadows and just listen. They could not speak to each other and must be as quiet as mice and not even shuffle their feet. So, the children prepared themselves to wait in silence while the important meeting took place.

The men sat and looked into the fire. Some smoked their pipes and stared into the fire. Others looked heavenward as if to learn the words the Great Spirit would have them speak. Finally, the chief of the west village cleared his throat and stood up. He said, "I will not speak my words now. There is one among us who has made this meeting happen at this time. We should hear from him. His village is east of my village, but in the center of our many lands. Many paths from our villages cross in the meadow near his village. He has brought us together. Let us hear from him." The other chiefs nodded their heads and made a sort of collective humming sound as they did.

Father stood up. He looked slowly from left to right around the circle, even moving around the flames to see each chief. As he did, he would give each chief a nod. Then he spoke. "Great chiefs, my friend, Demothi sits here with me. He knows many of your languages and will speak your words as I speak my words to help us all understand. The east village has a language that is unknown to most of us, but there is a man from the north village who understands and will use their words and then tell us the words of their chief." He motioned to the two interpreters. They stood and came forward. One now stood at his left side and the other to his right.

Father continued to speak. "This great council of chiefs is needed to find ways to help our tribes through the hard winter that is coming. We do not want our children to be hungry and die. We do not want to steal from each other. We do not want to make war and kill the fathers of these children. Our tribes have different ways. As more children are born each year, our tribes grow larger. More and more, our children will cross the paths of each other. If the ways of other tribes are strange to them, they will become enemies. If the ways of other tribes are familiar, they will become friends. We can help our children to live together in this wonderful land that has plenty of water and earth and antelope and bear and elk for all tribes. We must talk. We will learn the needs of each tribe. Tell us what you fear. Tell us what you want for your families."

There began to be whispering, then the talk among chiefs became louder. Tehya and Hakan could no longer hear Father's words. Soon, Father stepped up onto a rock near the edge of the fire and raised his hand high in the air. "We must not talk to the wind. We must talk to each other. Let each chief who wishes to speak come forward to this stone to tell us his words."

The chiefs became quiet. The first chief to stand on the rock proclaimed, "I think this visit to the west village is good for feasting and dancing, but it is foolish to believe we can have one way for all tribes. We must go to our own homes tomorrow and prepare for winter. If some tribes do not have enough, this is because of their foolishness. They will die like the squirrels who do not store nuts in their dens. We do not wish this for them, but we must take care of our own families first."

Another chief stood and rebuked the first chief. "Some villages do not have so much water as your village. Some have sickness and they did not choose this sickness. If there is extra corn and meat in my village, my people will give it to a village that is hungry. When the next winter comes, we may need corn or meat and they will share with us."

A third chief spoke, "We will feed our own children and stay in our own land. If someone comes to steal from our village, we have watchers who will see them. We will kill any thieves when they cross the poles that surround our village. These poles mark the land that is ours."

A frightening argument began to build. Individual chiefs stood up next to those who had been sitting beside them and turned with pointing fingers to say, "You are wrong. You do not understand. Your way will not work." The arguments were returned as: "You do not listen. Your people are too angry. Your way is not the way of the Great Spirit."

Tehya and Hakan particularly noticed when the one chief made this last remark about the Great Spirit. They wondered if the Great Spirit would argue as these men did. The chief who said these words leaned very close to the other chief's face. The chief who was being criticized suddenly reached out and pushed the other man backwards. They shouted at each other. Tehya and Hakan became frightened.

Father went to the fire with a torch light to ignite it. He then moved to the stone with his interpreters and stepped up waving the torch as he did. The chiefs immediately stopped arguing. Father spoke very loudly. "Great chiefs, our families are watching. The Great Spirit is watching. We are not listening to each other. We have the spirit of war not friendship. This is a time to walk away from the fire to find cool air and water. Then we will return. If any chief wishes to say his last words, come to me now and I will make a time for your speaking when we return."

The chiefs all walked quietly away from the fire. Tehya and Hakan sat still for a short time and then went to find water. As they walked along, Father found them. "Children, you must go to bed now. There is too much anger among the chiefs for children to watch. Go to bed."

Hakan spoke. "Father, I must learn from you. You will lead the chiefs and I must learn to lead."

Tehya added, "I know that what the chiefs say when they return will change our lives for many years to come. It is important for the children to understand the ways of their parents so we can help our parents. Let us listen."

"Tehya," said Father, "You and Hakan are only children. The chiefs are old and have learned many things. They must decide. This time is not for children."

"Father, we are children, but we know what the Great Spirit is thinking because we are young. We came from heaven not long ago. Some of the chiefs have forgotten what the Great Spirit taught us there."

"Tehya, you and Hakan may stay near the fire but without any sound. Do not move one finger or one toe or blink your eyes, do you understand?"

"Father, you are teasing us."

The children found water and returned to the forest's edge near the fire just as the chiefs were gathering. Father went alone toward the fire. One of the chiefs stopped him on his way. They spoke briefly. When he reached the fire, three more chiefs were waiting for him. They spoke together briefly as the meeting was about to reconvene.

There was silence. Father stood atop the stone near the fire. "Great chiefs, three of you have asked me to let the council hear their final words before we make a decision about the future of our land with its many tribes: the chief of the south village, the chief of the west village, and the chief of the east village. Also, while I was finding water and as I was walking back to our meeting, the chief of the north stopped me to say that his people have worked hard but do not have enough food and clothing for the winter. They are sad that we think of them as squirrels who did not store nuts. Sickness did come to them. And their water spring went dry at the end of summer. They have to walk very far to find water each day. This has made them tired and thin. They do not want war and will trade their stone knives and wooden tools for dried meat and nuts. They make very fine knives and tools. We should trade with them."

It was time for the meeting to proceed. Father introduced each of the three chiefs who wished to speak. These are their words…

Chief of the South Village

The chief walked confidently to the center of the fire circle and stepped up onto the stone to speak briefly.

"Our tribe has a good plan for many things. Our people talk together about many plans and tell me their thoughts before I decide what we will do. We have watchers who see any dangers that can come to our village—forest fires, wild animals, fierce storms, or thieves. We use poles to mark our land so that other tribes know which land belongs to us. We believe our way is best for all tribes. We will come to your villages and teach you our way so you will be more wise and able to protect your lands and your children. Then, we will have one way and no war."

Chief of the West Village

This chief was the large man. He arose very slowly. As he did, and from out of the dark, came six warriors stepping carefully between the pairs of chiefs seated side by side. The warriors walked softly and carried long spears. Their faces had white markings that glowed in the firelight. They looked fierce.

As Tehya and Hakan watched, Tehya turned to her brother and said, "I have many dreams and this is like a bad dream. These men scare me. What are they doing?"

The chief of the west village stood on the stone to speak. "You have come to my village. This was my plan. Our village is best because it is very large. We have the finest wood for our houses. We have been very wise and stored much food—enough to feed ourselves through the winter and to feed you as our guests. Of the many tribes, we are the strongest. My warriors stand before you for two reasons: first, they can protect you. They can protect all your villages. The second reason is to let you see that, if there are thieves or foolish people or those who would argue with us, we can stop you. We can control all things. Our way is best. If we must make a war with any of you, you will lose. If you are wise, you will listen to our way."

As this chief finished, two of his warriors came and stood next to him then escorted him back to his sitting place. All of the warriors gathered into one straight line and marched out of the fire circle, all holding their spears in the same position in their right hands.

Chief of the East Village

This chief walked slowly with his head bowed as if praying. Three men accompanied him. One was the interpreter from the north village. The other was a large man with black hair and a very thick, black beard. Tehya thought he was a handsome man but he looked angry. The third man also had a dark beard. He was smaller and stood in front of the larger man. Their chief spoke.

"We know of the Great Spirit you believe answers your prayers. We know this Great Spirit best of all. Our village honors this one you call God continuously. It is the will of God that all tribes follow our teachings and pray often."

The chief paused. The smaller of his two men kneeled down and began to pray. The larger man behind him stepped back as if to watch him pray. As he did, his white gown parted so that all could see a strange curved knife hanging from his waist. When the praying man finished, he stood up and the large man came closer. As he did, he covered up the knife at his side.

Tehya turned to Hakan and whispered. "Do you think the man with the knife was protecting the man who prayed or would he kill the man if he did not pray?"

"Tehya," Hakan whispered, "I do not know, but I would pray if that man were watching me. I would pray for courage if I should die."

The chief of the east continued. "Our people are a peace-loving people and we wish to provide food for the hungry people to the north. This is our way. It is the will of the Great Spirit for us. Our way is best for all tribes. It is the will of the Great Spirit."

The chief of the village to the east turned and walked away from the fire accompanied by his two men who then left the circle and disappeared into the dark. Their interpreter remained.

Father stood. These are his final words: "Great chiefs, whatever we decide, it is my prayer that we have been friends for these two or three days and will remember the dancing, the feasting, the singing, and the playing of our children. We thank the people of the west village for letting us be their guests. Their blankets are very soft and warm. Their food is abundant and well prepared. I believe we should go to our families now and meet once more when the sun comes up to make our decisions. Go now. Sleep well. You have spoken many wise things. We will all think on these things."

All the chiefs and their men were tired and walked slowly back to the houses where their families were waiting. Very few families were sleeping. All wondered about the important history that was being made.

A Time to Think and to Ask

Father walked to his children sitting in the dark in a small thicket of pine trees. He did not greet them or say any words. The children knew it was a thinking time for him. With Hakan on his right and Tehya on his left, he put his arms around their necks as they walked together back to their guesthouse where Mother was waiting patiently as Yepa slept.

Once inside, Father motioned for the family to gather around him. He looked sad, sadder than Tehya ever remembered seeing him. "My family, this is a night of much worry for me. The chiefs have many strong ideas. They do not listen to each other. I am afraid some love their spears, their lands, their own plans, and their prayer rituals more than they love peace."

There was silence for a short time. Mother spoke. "Father, you have done all that you can do. The Great Spirit must help us now."

Tehya was full of many thoughts that were buzzing around inside her head like a honey bee circling its hive. She was trying to find the right thought for Father. She started to speak and then the honey bee inside her head began to buzz again. She was confused. Finally, she could only ask a question. She asked it with much careful thought. **"Father, who owns the world?"**

Father was also full of many thoughts and did not hear her question. "What did you say, daughter?"

"Father, who owns the world?" Does one chief own the world because he is a large man and has many warriors with tall spears and fine wood for his houses? Must we follow his way because he can make war on us and control us? Does one chief own the world because he has so many plans and watchers and poles to mark his lands? Because he is smart and can teach us, do we have to take his way and throw away

90

the teachings of our ancestors? Does one chief own the world because his people pray more often? If we do not pray his way, will his men kill us and tell us it is the will of the Great Spirit? Father, who owns the world? Does the Great Spirit own the world?"

A Time to Think and to Answer

Father was staring into the eyes of his young daughter. He remembered what she had said earlier. Now, it had special meaning. Yes, his daughter did still remember what the Great Spirit would be thinking. She had come from heaven not long ago. The chiefs were wise but not so wise as a child can sometimes be.

"Tehya, this is my thinking. God is the Great Spirit and the Great Chief of all tribes. God has made this world with all its earth, water, trees, flowers, clouds, honey bees, antelope, and other wondrous things for all tribes to use and to enjoy. It is not an accident that we are all here—all tribes. God placed all of us here. The will of God is for us to all learn, to work hard, to be strong, to love our families, and to help each other. God could be the owner of this world, but God has decided to give the world to us. You ask who owns the world. We do. All of us own the world. I do, you do, and Hakan, Yepa, Mother, our tribe, the tribe to the north and the west and the south and the east. Tehya, you own the world; together we all own the world. There is not one tribe that can tell another tribe that their way is the only way. Each way came from our ancestors for a purpose. Each tribe has much good to share with other tribes. One tribe can build beautiful houses, another tribe makes fine tools, and another tribe knows how to plan for the future. Each tribe wants snow in the mountains to keep our water springs flowing through the summer. Each tribe wants healthy children who will work and follow the ways of their parents and grandparents."

Mother was listening as she always did so well. When she spoke it was usually with softness and with firmness when needed. "My husband, you are a good man. Hakan, you will become like your father. Tehya, you shine more brightly than this beautiful stone your father placed around my neck. As you speak, we know what the Great Spirit is thinking. These are my thoughts. Let me tell you a simple story. It was at summer's end. I remember walking along the path north of our village. I stopped to adjust my carry sack. As I did, I looked at my feet and saw ants crawling over them. Some bit my feet. The ants had been using the same path I was using. At first I was angry with the ants and stomped my feet. Then I began walking with the ants under my feet hoping to kill some of them as punishment for biting my feet. After a moment, I stepped aside into the tall grass and looked down at the ants once again. I spoke to the ants and said, 'You are busy doing your work in your way. I am busy and going to do my work in my own way. I will not step on you if you will not bite my feet.' I continued walking alongside the ants. Some tribes wish to step on other tribes when they can walk alongside each other in their own ways without biting each other."

Father smiled. Tehya smiled. Hakan had leaned backward and was now fast asleep. Father looked lovingly at Tehya and asked, "Child, oh wise child, what would you do with the chiefs in the morning?"

A Council of Mothers

Tehya did not hesitate in responding to her father's profound inquiry. "I have a plan, Father." She paused just briefly to collect her thoughts. "Early in the morning, Mother can go to the wife of the chief of this village to thank her and to give her a special gift. Then, these two mothers—one who is your wife, wife of the leader of the great council meeting, and the other mother who is the wife of the chief of this village where we are guests—can become the leaders of women. They will go to invite the wives of the other chiefs to attend a great *council of mothers*. The women will meet while the chiefs are having breakfast. Together, they will decide what mothers believe will help the chiefs with their decisions.

"Father, as the chiefs are preparing to have their breakfast, you will tell them that the mothers have asked to speak before them as they make their final decisions about the future of our families. If the men do not want to hear the women speak or if they laugh, you must be strong and tell them that the women will not take a long time to speak and that the Great Spirit wants the mothers to speak because they have brought the children from heaven who will care for the chiefs when they are old."

"Tehya, this is dangerous. The chiefs do not want mothers or children or other men telling them what to do. And, what gift will Mother give to the wife of the chief of this village?"

Mother spoke next, "Father, tell the chiefs we will not tell them what they must do. We will tell them simple ideas that will help them to think of the right things to do. Perhaps there will be just one or two useful ideas to guide them as they make their decisions."

"Mother, Father, I know the gift," said Tehya. "You have both told me that when I find my husband, Mother will give me the shiny stone that you gave her, Father. I do not have

94

a husband to love now. I am too young. What I love now is for there to be peace among the tribes. Mother can give my shiny stone to the wife of the west village chief. When we return to our village, you will find a new stone for Mother to give to me one day. This one stone can change our history if the chiefs will listen to the mothers. This is my small way to help, Father."

Father pondered. "This is too much now. I am too tired. Let's go to sleep. When we awake in the morning, we will know what to do." Father reached over and stroked the silky, black hair of his two beautiful women. "I love you both. Good night."

A Bright New Day

The night before this new day was the longest night of the year. With the new day, winter had begun and the sky was again blue. The air was crisp. A hawk was circling over the west village making so much noise for such a small animal. Tehya sat up and peeked out the window of their guest house then quickly turned around to see if Mother was there. Mother was gone and so was Father. Yepa was sleeping next to Hakan. She knew a very important day had begun.

The chiefs had all arisen early. They knew there would be a final council meeting, followed by much preparation for their journeys home. Father had quickly made the rounds of all the guesthouses where the chiefs stayed. They had agreed to a special preparatory meeting with him just before breakfast and were now gathering at the house of their host, the chief of the west village. In front of the house was a circle of logs. The men crowded around in this circle that was much smaller than the one that surrounded the large council fire.

Father thanked the chiefs for their willingness to meet early. He explained that there had been an unusual request made by his wife that she might have an opportunity to meet with their wives briefly as a council of mothers. The women wished to give the chiefs their thoughts about the upcoming winter situation and their concern for the children. He promised the chiefs that the mothers would meet as soon as the children were fed and while the chiefs were enjoying their breakfast. The women would prepare to give the chiefs a short and simple report at the beginning of the tribal council meeting. Then, all families could begin their journeys back to their own villages. Father told the chief of the west that their two wives were working together to organize the council of mothers. The large man had been frowning with what appeared to be a look of disapproval. Upon learning of his wife's involvement, his countenance softened. He said, "This is good, but the women must understand that the chiefs will decide what is best for all tribes. We will decide." Father agreed.

Mother had managed to locate the west chief's wife and they were strolling together in the center of the village. Mother offered to give her new friend the beautiful, shiny stone that had been her treasure for several years. She explained the need for support in finding a way to involve the other mothers and to have their voices heard by the chiefs. The wife of the west chief declined the gift. She said, "You and your husband are very wise and very kind. It is already a gift that you have traveled so far to visit our village. Thank you." She continued, "I am concerned that my husband and some of the other chiefs will not want to hear what the mothers say about this very big problem facing our people or perhaps they will pretend to listen and it will be a waste of our time to meet and to talk as mothers."

Mother encouraged her in this way. "My friend, if the chiefs listen, it will be a good thing. If they do not, the mothers will have become friends. We will be ready to help our husbands when problems do come—when the winter hunger comes. There may be stealing and the tribes will become angry with each other. The strength of women will be needed in all villages."

The two women walked together a little longer. Tehya saw them. They were nodding and smiling. Then they separated to the two sides of the village and began knocking on the doors of the houses where the chiefs and their families had slept. A council of mothers was about to happen.

The council of mothers included 10 women. There would have been 11, but the wife of the chief of the east village was not able to attend and sent her regrets to the rest of the women. She asked that they send a messenger to her guesthouse with their decisions and that she would send a messenger in return with her thoughts.

The meeting of the mothers was different than the meeting of chiefs. Individual women took turns telling of their fears and their hopes. They also talked about their husbands, the chiefs. They knew the men needed to be powerful and to protect their people. As mothers, they, too, needed to protect—to protect their children. They did not want their children to be hungry or angry with each other. And they did not want their children to see the blood of death. If they did, they would have bad dreams for many years to come. Most of all, they wanted their children to know peace—to understand the original beauty of the world God had created for them.

After the women had spoken together for a time, Mother asked for a decision of the most important things to tell their husbands and perhaps one idea, above all others, which the men could easily remember as they made their decisions. She reminded the women of her promise to not tell the men what to do but to give them ideas that would guide their thinking.

The women succeeded in agreeing on a list of "What Mothers Believe." Mother volunteered to be the messenger to visit the guesthouse where the wife of the east village chief was waiting and to include her in their decision. This she did as the other women returned to their children.

The Time of Decisions

The chiefs had already gathered and were waiting for the report from the council of mothers. Mother had been chosen to speak for them. She now stood in the circle of men that surrounded the morning fire. The chiefs had stepped aside and made way for her. She was a lone woman among these tall warriors and mighty chiefs. She looked to her left and to her right. Some of the chiefs were young and very handsome. Some were old and wrinkled with gray hair and still handsome in their old way. Only a few chiefs smiled. The others looked impatient. She knew she had to speak clearly and with few words. This is her message to the great tribal council.

"Great chiefs, I stand with you as a humble member of my own village who honors our chief, who is my husband. Like all of you, he is wise. He also listens to my thoughts. For this, I am very grateful. I thank you for this short time to listen to the thoughts of your wives. We come to you without the authority of great chiefs but with the authority of those who carry unborn children and who bring new life to each village. Without this new life, each village would die and the ways of our tribes would be no more. We know there is a hard winter coming. There may be thieves and the tribes would be angry with each other. We cannot make the important decisions about what our many tribes must do, but we can tell you of our beliefs and one great idea to guide your thinking. This is what the mothers believe.

"We believe that all tribes have the right to protect those who live in their villages and to protect the way their ancestors have taught them.

"We believe that no tribe has the right to invade another tribe to threaten them, to steal from them, or to force them to change the way they live in their own land.

"We believe that each tribe has special gifts to share with other tribes. We can learn of each other as we understand these gifts. We can trade gifts of food, clothing, knives, wood, stones, and many other things so that all tribes can give what is theirs to give, where there is plenty. Other tribes can receive what they do not have, which they will need to survive the winter and protect their children.

"We believe we can have peace and there is one important idea to help guide your thoughts and your decisions. Yesterday, a child of the east village became lost. For that time while the child was lost, we all became as one large tribe. With all of the beautiful houses that surrounded us in this village and all the mighty warriors with their spears ready to protect the village and with the dancing and music and feasting that we have enjoyed, for that time while the child was lost, we all knew one thing above all other things. It is the importance of one child. This is our thought to guide the thinking of our great chiefs: **Do what is best for our children**—for each child in each village in every land. This is our one most important idea. Thank you."

Chiefs Agree, but Only Faintly See

The chiefs stood silently as Mother left the circle. Father moved to the center of the circle and asked that they be seated. The men met briefly and these are their final decisions.

The chiefs determined that there could not be just one big plan for all the problems the many tribes might experience in the coming months, but there could be another great tribal council meeting if these needs became very large. Perhaps they could talk before any tribe would make a war.

They agreed that the village to the north and other smaller villages would need more food for the winter. Any tribe that had extra food would take it to the village where the many paths crossed. They acknowledged Father as a fair and honest chief. He would decide who was most hungry and send the food where it would be needed most.

The chiefs did agree that there had been too many wars as told in the stories of their ancestors, but that wars are necessary when the ways of tribes are too different and there is too much anger for talking. Therefore, war spears would still be necessary and the making of spears would keep many men busy between hunting expeditions and until the spring planting. The making of spears is a good work to prepare for war and for trading with other tribes. The chiefs of the smaller tribes objected to this idea because they did not have enough men for making spears or enough of the right stones for making the spearheads. The larger tribes promised to provide them with spears in exchange for animal hides, tools, fine wood, and other things.

Returning Home with Hope and Fear

As the many families prepared for their journeys, there was a sense of history and a sense of hope mixed with worry. All hoped that there would be peace. They also hoped that some angry or foolish chief would not forget the original beauty of their lives, stir the thoughts of anger and tribal warfare, and forget what is best for their children.

As Tehya and her family left the village, she walked alongside her father. She reached out and took his hand. She looked up at him and briefly studied his face. "Father, you are worried. You do not believe the chief of the west. He has too many warriors with too many spears. The ways of the east village are very strange. I think their people are good people but they do not want to belong to one great tribe and share the land. These things make you worry, Father, I know."

"Child, you have the wisdom of an owl. We do not know what will happen."

"Father, there is one force stronger than the spears of many warriors."

"What is that Tehya?"

"It is the love of parents for their children."

"But, Tehya, the parents of each village want to teach their children their own ways and do not care about the children of other villages."

"Father, you must remind them that a great war will kill fathers from every village. Their children will all see the blood of death. Without fathers, there will be no hunting and there will not be enough meat for any of the villages. Then, we will suffer and we will cry for all the people who suffer with us. Father, what will harm even one child will become larger and larger to harm all the children in all the world. There will be much fear and much anger. Children will no longer be as children. Their smiles will be gone. They will show the anger of their parents in their faces. The original beauty of the world will be gone. Father, we must tell this story to every family who walks along the many paths that cross in the meadow near our village. We must remind them to tell their chiefs to do what is best for all the children."

"Tehya, this will become your story. You must teach it to the other children. It is the story only a child can tell. You tell it well, my daughter. I will pray to the Great Spirit that many will listen."

Conclusion

Among the villages Tehya knew, her perceptions were not of *bad* people, *strange* people, or *good* people. In each village, there were people with families and houses and their special *gifts*. They tended their corn fields, picked berries, and hunted the antelope, elk, and bear. There were men and women and children. Among them were those whose hearts were filled with anger and many more whose hearts were full of kindness. There were those with many needs and those who had plenty. And each tribe had their own way, which the other tribes may have thought to be a strange way.

When the people of her village and the neighboring villages traded their *gifts*, helped each other through the hard winters, and did what was best for the children, there was peace. When there was peace, there was a learning of the ways of other tribes and their ancestors. Then the ways of others were not strange. Spears would hang on their hooks, except for hunting. There was no war.

As Tehya grew older, the shiny stone that once hung around her mother's neck became her own. She remembered the great council of mothers and her wisdom grew. She held on to hope. Many villages called her *teacher*.

This is what Tehya learned. This is what she taught. This is what she prayed her people would remember.

For every drought that comes,
Ten thousand fields of grain have grown.
For every war that raged,
Ten thousand acts of kindness shown.

Epilogue

Century Number 21: What Do You Believe?

The last the world will ever see?
A time of strife and toil and danger everywhere;
A time of pleasure.
New horizons to explore, more to learn than time,
A test of skill and courage and compassion;
An opportunity that is mine.

Never in all of history has there been the combination of technologies, resources, and know-how that could so positively alter the course of human events. We have the potential to eliminate poverty, ignorance, devastating diseases, and political oppression. Our opportunity is unprecedented and astonishing. We cannot afford distractions. It is time for a conversation about what is best for our children.

-Darby Checketts

www.ingramcontent.com/pod-product-compliance
Lightning Source LLC
Chambersburg PA
CBHW031839170626
46807CB00004B/1527